THE CASE
— of the —
CANTERFELL
CODICIL

The first *Anty Boisjoly* Mystery

Copyright 2020 PJ Fitzsimmons.
All Rights Reserved.

THE CASE — of the — CANTERFELL CODICIL

1. The Enigmatic Encounter on the 16:42 from Charing Cross..................1
2. The Perplexing Path of the Forgetful Footman..................11
3. The Pertinence of the Improbable Parable..................23
4. The Main Course Mystery..................34
5. The Lofty Window of the Loaded Widow..................47
6. The Mystery of the Missing Muse..................61
7. The Affair of the Abayant Earldom..................73
8. The Puzzle of the Purloined Poison Pen..................85
9. The Conundrum of the Confrontation on the Khyber Pass..................96
10. The Continuing Consequences of the Norman Conquest..................110
11. The Suspicious Circumstance of the Sealed Study..................122
12. The Spectacular Spectacle of the Susceptible Spectacles..................135
13. The Inscrutable Nature of the English Summer..................145
14. The Frightful Fate of the Fourth Earl of Fray..................158
15. The Puzzling Case of the Puzzling Case..................167
16. The Intriguing Identity of Powderkeg Malone..................175
17. The Obscure Origins of Quite Right, Milord..................187
18. The Momentous Meaning of the Major's Mistaken Memories..................194
19. The Contents of the Canterfell Codicil..................203
20. The Tantalising Twist in the Case of the Canterfell Codicil..................211

Anty Boisjoly Mysteries..................218

CHAPTER ONE

The Enigmatic Encounter on the 16:42 from Charing Cross

"COME AT ONCE -(STOP)- UNCLE SEB. DEAD -(STOP)- DEFENESTRATED BY UNSEEN HAND -(STOP)- FIDDLES"

"Rummy missive," I said to Carnaby, steward of the Juniper Gentleman's Club. He'd just read the telegram aloud for my benefit, my hands being otherwise occupied with a whisky and soda syphon. "What do you make of it?"

"I would hazard that someone of your acquaintance has been pushed from a window by a person or persons unknown, sir." Carnaby gleaned this without so much as touching the paper, which he carried on a doily on a pewter salver.

"You're quite certain it's for me, Carnaby?" I asked, reclining now with my bracer in a worn leather armchair of a species native to deep, burgundy-toned salons with rosewood wainscotting and high, paned windows giving onto a clattering street in Mayfair.

"It was addressed to Mister Anthony Boisjoly, sir."

Which was compelling, if not positively conclusive. Boisjoly is rarely pronounced correctly (it's "Boo-juhlay", for the record, like the wine region) but it's equally rarely mistaken for, say, Jones. I'm also hard to miss, at the Juniper, being the only dashing young rake with a full head of chestnut locks in a sea of dozing grey noggins for as far as the salon stretches in any direction.

"Damning," I confessed. "Best hand it over."

A glance at the postmark brought the entire picture into sharp focus. The telegram was sent that very day — July 12, 1928 — from the post office in Fray, East Sussex.

"Got it in one, Carnaby," I said. "The dearly departed in question is one Sebastian Canterfell."

"May I offer you my condolences, sir." Carnaby made his eyebrows bow solemnly, as only a club steward can.

"You may, Carnaby, so long as you don't mind me pocketing them for later consumption. I barely knew the man. I was at school with his nephew, Fairfax, better known to you as Fiddles, author of this exercise in cryptography."

"Please extend the commiseration of the Juniper."

"Will do," I assured him. "If you'll just conjure me a taxi, I'll be expressing your inexpressible sorrow before sunset."

During that time, anyone who knew me even slightly also knew that my life revolved around the Juniper. I was between valets, the most recent of an unbroken string of disasters ending with a fire in my flat that could be seen from Hampstead, and I was staying at the club until my affairs were in order. So an invitation to visit Canterfell Hall, circumstances aside, came as a welcome change of pace.

The Juniper is a capital club with a wine list to rival the Ritz and a Carnaby who could out-steward all challengers, but I know from several languid summers down from Oxford that the Canterfell pile is dripping with the poetry of the English countryside. It's one of those majestic scatterings of ramparts and barbicans occupying the headlands of a thatched village, itself preserved in aspic immediately upon tidying up after the War of the Roses.

Furthermore, the place is a positive embarrassment of luxury and decadence, with no expense spared in the thankless pursuit of impressing classmates of first-born sons. In the days of my youth, Canterfell Hall had a kitchen staff imported wholesale from France, including a dedicated wine steward who had once refused to serve King George a Chablis with his *gigot d'agneau en croûte*.

In the absence of a valet, I was forced to pack by process of looking at myself in a mirror and endeavouring to reproduce the effect in a satchel, four or five times over. This had the single happy side-effect of being quickly done, and I was at Charing Cross with enough time to spare for the 16:42 to Hastings that I was able to dash off a telegram to Fiddles, warning of my arrival.

It was one of those rich, sun-splashed afternoons, custom ordered for a journey by train and made all the more glorious by two whisky-sodas and the Surrey countryside chugging past, smelling of apple blossoms and coal dust. Nevertheless, I was pleased when, just after departure, the door to my otherwise lonesome compartment rattled open and a chap with a military bearing and suspicious moustache looked in and said "Hastings?" I leapt at the opportunity, of course, and sprang to my feet and offered him my hand.

"No," I said, "Boisjoly."

Sometimes spontaneous wit serves as a roaring great icebreaker, sometimes it falls to the floor of the first-class compartment with a clang. It's in the delivery, I expect. I blame myself.

"No," said the chap, after a moment of uncertainty for which I feel partially responsible. "Is this the train to Hastings?"

I confirmed that it was and invited my travel companion to take the seat across from me, but he chose the place nearest the door. Doubtless he suffered from motion sickness. In addition to a moustache that looked like an act of petty vandalism, the poor chap appeared to be wearing everything he owned on a hot afternoon in mid-July. I felt overdressed in a cotton driving suit and, were I alone, I'd have been sorely tempted to loosen my tie. Yet here was this fellow in a trench coat sort of affair in sidewalk grey, and low-brimmed fedora in the American style. In short, he was a mystery, and I knew without knowing why that he was going to play some role in the adventure which was about to unfold.

He was poring over a folder of hand-written notes on yellow paper, and studiously ignoring all manner of overture from an explicit "ahem" to my most seductive "hot, isn't it?", and so I resorted to a frontal attack.

"Anthony Boisjoly, that is," I said, again offering my hand. Whatever else he may have been, he was an English gentleman, and so was left with no choice but to sigh like a commuter and shake my hand.

"Ivor Wittersham," he pronounced himself.

"Oh yes?" I said. "Of the Wittersham Wittershams?"

"Distantly," answered Ivor, with what I thought briefly might have been a hint of impatience.

"Giles Wittersham — Lord Tisham, now, if memory serves — was a year ahead of me at Oxford. Sent down for absconding with university property. He was selling Magdalen Chapel hymn books to tourists. One shilling six.

Two shillings even if you wanted him to sign *'Compliments of Baron Davidson of Lambeth, Archbishop of Canterbury'* on the inside front cover."

"You don't say," said Ivor.

"I do say," I confirmed. "A gross overreaction on the part of the college, in my view — the poor man was practically destitute. The family came out of the war with a title and little else. Invested heavily in Austro-Hungarian war bonds, I believe. Hard luck, for Lord Tisham, at any rate. Could have gone either way."

Ivor stared at me with no expression, as though I had faded to transparency during my monologue and he was looking through me at the passing greenery.

"So," I said at last, breaking the vigil. "Do you know Hastings well? I can recommend the castle, while it lasts; it was in a deplorable state when I was there in '25."

"I'm not going to Hastings," said Ivor. "I'm stopping at Fray."

"That's a coincidence," I said, despite a looming suspicion that it was nothing of the sort. "So am I."

"Do you know Fray, as well?"

"Intimately," I said. "It's the country seat of an old college chum, Fairfax Canterfell."

"Any relation?" asked Ivor, referring to Fairfax's father who sat, at the time, on the Conservative benches in Parliament.

"Beloved offspring to the honourable member and his late, lamented wife," I said. "We called him Fiddlesticks, for Fairfax, and we called him Fairfax because his real name is Evelyn."

"Seems a perfectly respectable name," observed Ivor.

"Very respectable indeed," I agreed. "But Fairfax had a

cousin at school at the same time — Evelyn Harold Canterfell."

"Whom you called, I assume, Harold."

"Hal, actually, but you're in the right lane."

"And you're calling on your old school friend? On a whim?"

There was something decidedly fishy about the way my new acquaintance spoke the word 'whim' as though it was underlined, and I felt a justifiable impulse to defend my impulsiveness.

"Hardly," I said, coolly. "I have been invited. Urgently, I might add. There's been a death in the family. The above-mentioned Hal's father, as it happens — Sebastian Canterfell."

"What is it that you do, Mister Boisjoly?" asked Ivor.

"Do? I flit, mainly, between club and theatre. I'm what the French would call a *flaneur*, if they knew me."

"So you're not a mortician then."

"A mortician?" I said. "No, hardly. I gave a famously moving eulogy at my father's funeral last year, parts of which were printed in the Times. They left out the funniest lines, in my view, but that's modern journalism for you. And that's the closest I've come to that noble undertaking, if you'll forgive the pun."

"A notary of some sort? Probate attorney?"

"Ah, I see what you're driving at," I said, the mists clearing. "No, I've been asked to look in because there's apparently something quite peculiar in the manner of the passing of Sebastian Canterfell."

"Oh, I see," said Ivor. "You're a police officer."

"Oh my dear lord no," I scoffed. "Not at all. Too much regard for my fellow man, I think. But I do enjoy a modest reputation among my kin and kind as something of a problem-solver. The one to whom they turn in times of turmoil. The Alexander to their Gordian knots."

"Including death under mysterious circumstances?"

"Not as a rule, no," I confessed. "Usually more matters of the heart, domestic disputes, that sort of thing. Did you read of the engagement earlier this year of Elspeth Finch-Epping to Milton Entwhistle Hardy?"

"No."

"No? Well, you never would, either, had I not intervened when Milton — we called him Melting at school, obviously — when Milton was sued for breach of promise by a music-hall performer who went by the stage name of Iva Gudden, if you will."

"Bought her off, did you?" said Ivor, as though the practice of buying off music-hall singers was a late omen of the fall of man.

"Hardly," I said. "No, I proposed to Miss Gudden myself."

"Didn't that just transfer the problem to you?"

"A problem shared is a problem halved," I said. "Or, in this instance, divided by eleven, the sum total of all the men to whom Miss Gudden was engaged. When she sued me, too, for breach of promise, I was able to establish to the satisfaction of Elspeth and, above all, her mother, that Melting was the victim of a serial confidence trickster."

"So this will be your first murder."

"I'd hardly call it mine."

"Seems more a matter for the authorities," observed Ivor.

"Doubtless they'll be informed in due course," I said. "But you know how the police approach these things, arresting the first person who can't prove that he was in the company of two vicars at the time of the murder. It's a matter of incentive, you see. A career in law enforcement is built not on the number of guilty men hanged, merely the number of men hanged."

"Is that a fact?"

"Take it from me," I said. "The police will kick down the doors, arrest the footman and the gardener and, time permitting, the cook, and whichever had a grudge against the deceased and/or fails to account for his whereabouts wins a twine necktie."

"I expect that police procedure is marginally more complicated than that."

"Not by much," I said, warming to the theme. "The Canterfell family is tremendously wealthy, you see. Plodders find that intimidating. They'll be anxious to pin the affair on the lowest born pigeon. Drop an 'H' in close proximity to a cadaver of the ruling class and you'll be in the Clink before you can say 'garden gate'."

"Garden gate?"

"Magistrate. It's Cockney," I elucidated. "But forget you heard it. You'll want to stay well clear of rhyming slang if ever questioned by an English policeman regarding your disposition at the time his lordship was biffed in the back of the head with a brass candlestick holder."

"Was this Canterfell chap a lord?"

"I was speaking hypothetically," I explained. "No, the Canterfell name is currently without noble ornamentation. But the family own most of the village and surrounding field and glen."

"Ah," said Ivor. "So you think the killer is closer to home. A family member, no doubt."

"I don't like to express an opinion before getting a firm handle on the facts," I said. "I merely mean that one should approach this thing, as with all things, with an open mind. Might have been the gardener, might equally have been

Laetitia Canterfell, the dead man's wife, or his son, Hal."

"Or your friend, Fairfax?"

"In a pinch. Speaking very frankly, Sebastian Canterfell was not widely hailed as a fellow well-met."

"Disliked, was he?"

"In places far and near. I met a man by chance in the bar car of a train from Paris to Marseille who, unprompted, compared Sebastian Canterfell unfavourably to rubella."

"Unloved and wealthy. It seems open and shut."

"That's just what I expect the police will say," I said. "But the treasure remains in the hands of the family patriarch, Evelyn Clarence Canterfell. We call him the major."

"So who benefits from the death of Sebastian Canterfell?"

"There are those who would argue that we all do, in our way," I said. "But his brother, Halliwell, right honourable member for Fray, seems to fit the bill. Except that he's in Westminster as we speak, and in my own personal experience the man has all the penetrating intelligence of a country cabbage."

"Indeed?" said Ivor, doubtfully. "His speeches in parliament are famous."

"I daresay they are," I agreed. "He frequently stands up in support of measures not currently under consideration by His Majesty's government. Only this month, while the house debated the pensions act, he held the chamber spellbound for forty-five minutes on the subject of a national mollusc. I believe that he was agitating on behalf of the Selsey Cockle."

The train from London to Hastings traces a wide arc through dense woodland before passing through Tunbridge Wells, and it was in that instant that it broke free of a canopy of summer leaves and the evening sun burst into our compartment like a Roman candle. Ivor seized the opportunity to avert his eyes and return to his notes, and I contented myself with counting down the Victorian-era red brick station houses until the village of Fray, just this side of Hastings.

Only Ivor and I alighted at Fray, and there was nobody waiting to board. This is considered heavy traffic for the little station, which owes its existence to a proposed junction line between Bognor Regis and points East, an initiative that has so far not broken ground. At the village side of the station was a dusty Morris Cowley, with the top town and an Oxford chum leaning idly against the boot, smoking a cigarette.

Fiddles hadn't changed a bit since our days in college, apart from a monastic bald spot which got its start in his senior year, and the filling out of a tendency toward jowliness that he'd exhibited all his life. The result was a pleasant pudginess that somehow made him look younger every year. Doubtless in his dotage he would resemble a toddler. He was dressed as the gentleman farmer he'd become, all hobnails and shooting tweed.

"Anty," he said. "Thanks for coming so quickly, old man." We shook hands vigorously, not having clapped eyes on one another for over a year. Then he took in Ivor with a quizzical glance and said, "Inspector Wittersham, I presume."

CHAPTER TWO
The Perplexing Path of the Forgetful Footman

"Pleasure," said Ivor, taking and releasing Fiddles' hand. "Evelyn Fairfax, is it?"

"None other," said Fiddles. "Call me Fairfax. It'll be easier. My cousin is on hand as well, you see..."

"And his name is also Evelyn," interjected Ivor. "Yes, Mister Boisjoly has made a most informative travel companion."

I protested this breach of etiquette with both hands firmly on my hips, but the inspector affected to not notice and instead took the liberty of the passenger seat, his carpetbag on his lap. Fiddles put my satchel in the boot and in a moment we were bouncing down the country lane that passed for a main street in the medieval village of Fray.

Little had changed about the town since I saw it last some ten years prior. The drainage ditch looked new, and that level crossing sign was closer to the railway tracks, when last seen. Apart from these bold intrusions of the modern world, Fray remained as bucolic and charming as any market town in East Sussex and beyond. There was the obligatory 15th-century parish church dedicated to Saint George, with a pagan foundation and overgrown cemetery. The blacksmith's barn still gamely applied generations-old expertise in horse and carriage to automotive repair. Ivy-covered cottages with chaotic English gardens were as far apart as any two blocks in London.

"We've put you up at the inn," said Fiddles to Ivor as we passed The Hare's Foot, the only inn, as well as the only tavern, in the village. I knew it well, as a tavern at least, or more precisely as the dispenser of an excellent local bitter. It's a proper old-world hostelry, with a thatched roof and walls of cut stone. The original building, now much extended and improved, probably billeted soldiers during the Norman Conquest.

Woodland closed over the road just after the inn and then opened onto the vast grounds of Canterfell Hall. The castle and all its glory hove into view like a curtain opening on the coronation scene in Richard III, and somewhere trumpets seemed to play.

The estate was hilly and wooded and charmingly unkempt, like a quaint English garden that had been allowed to grow to the size of an eighteen-hole golf course with water hazard. The main building fit neatly into the rolling landscape, as though springing from it or being absorbed into it, wrapped in ivy and perched at the top of a rising and surrounded by a moat of verdant grasses, pebbly paths, flowering shrubbery, and sentries of wide, weepy oak trees. The manor itself had the eccentric aesthetic of the perennially reconstructed — its remaining tower a relic from the castle's days as a pawn of the realm of Ethelred the Unready, the porte-cochere entrance the last remains of the gothic manor dating from sometime in the middle ages, and the mansion itself, built by the wealth of the eastern empire in the early 1800s.

Now, one hundred years on, the inconsistent architecture had settled into a sort of ornate, organic unity with its surroundings. It had been three hundred years since the castle had last been asked to defend itself, and peace settled upon it naturally. The woods were lush, the grass was green and flowing, birds sang freely in the old-growth trees, and bees buzzed busily among the flowers, both domestic and wild.

"Fire the gardeners?" I asked Fiddles, with blunt reference to the green and flowing grasses.

"Most of them, yes," said Fiddles. "Uncle Sebastian's idea. He replaced them with a goat."

"I didn't realise they were that clever," I said. "Are goats good with topiary?"

"They're dumb as rocks, actually. I think the idea is that they'd graze on the lawns, keeping the grass in check, and eliminating the need to have it trimmed once a week."

Fiddles steered us through the open gate onto the long drive to the house. The gravel crunched beneath the wheels of the car in a most satisfying fashion.

"That's what infuriated him most — the recurring cost," continued Fiddles. "The gardens are trimmed and, a week later, they have to be done again. I expect it's why he was so happy to have gone bald."

"The goat doesn't seem to be keeping its end of the bargain."

"It did, at first, but they have no sense of loyalty, among a number of other serious character flaws. They wander off, you see, in search of greener pastures."

"Hard to imagine there are any," I said. We were within

the gardens, now, and accosted on all sides by dense grasslands.

"I take it Constable Pennybun has secured the scene," said Ivor, in a manner suggestive of one who has heard quite enough talk of goats.

"Is Hug Pennybun still the town bobby?" I said with a full heart.

"He is," said Fiddles, my joy shared in his voice. "And still a stout sentry of the life and liberty of a grateful village. He's got a bicycle now, and the station has a telephone."

Constable Hugh "Hug" Pennybun had entirely the wrong temperament to be a police officer anywhere but a town like Fray where, until today, the most serious offence committed was public drunkenness, and even then only when Fiddles and I were down from Oxford. He knew every resident by name and he knew what they liked to drink and in spite, or perhaps because of, his intimate familiarity with all things Fray, Hug maintained the hard, cynical shell of a novitiate nun. He believed in the fundamental goodness of all people and he could turn a blind eye to anything that contradicted that happy world view with the reflexes of a cat.

The car crunched to a halt in front of the porte-cochere entrance.

"You'll have to manage your own bags, I'm afraid," said Fiddles. "We're on a skeleton staff. Butler, footman, cook, maid, and occasional scullery. And the one remaining gardener. It's how I imagine living on a deserted island would be."

"Has the family fallen on hard times, Fiddles?" I asked, helping myself to the boot.

"Not to my knowledge," said Fiddles. "The old man is withdrawing a bit from the family affairs — he's eighty-two, you know — and Uncle Sebastian had sort of taken over."

The main hall of the place was showing signs of neglect similar to those of the garden. It was still magnificent, of course, with marble floors and brass knobs, fixtures, fittings, and finery, and twin staircases to the respective wings, complete with portraits of Canterfell scoundrels climbing the walls. From the spartan ground floor of the ancient tower, the entrance hall had evolved into a grand baroque lobby, and it was the only thoroughfare connecting the wings to each other and the drawing-room, and the dining room beyond. All that remained of the original interior design was the centrepiece — an enormous fireplace, suitable for spit-roasting a mastodon.

But there was an unaccustomed dullness to it all that stood in stark contrast to the shining, loud, luxurious, bright and brilliantly lit Canterfell Hall of my carefree youth. There was a thin but telling layer of dust on the once gleaming fixtures. The marble tiles had lost the lustre of yesteryear, when you could see your face in them. There was a cobweb in the chandelier.

The most marked difference, of course, was measured in population density. On previous visits, the reception committee would be legion and number among them butlers, footmen, maids and fawning parents, two by two. Now, without including Fiddles, Ivor, and yours truly, the foyer was empty.

Fiddles smiled awkwardly, like a chap who's insisted on picking up the check just before realising that he's left his wallet elsewhere. Then he inhaled deeply, as he did in his coxswain days in prelude to a robust "Let it glide!" and instead bellowed something that sounded like "Lid!"

Satisfied with his delivery, Fiddles returned his energies to his awkward smile until the arrival of a weedy chap in an ill-fitting suit that might be called butler attire, were it to be worn by a butler. This fellow, however, was unshaven and unpolished, in a manner much like the house and grounds, and he pronounced "Sir?" with a tone that miraculously transformed the word into "What now?"

"Ah, Lydde," said Fiddles. "This is Mister Boisjoly and Inspector Wittersham."

Lydde crossed his arms in a manner which said "What of it?" as clearly as if he'd spoken the words aloud.

"Would you show Mister Boisjoly to the Blue Room?" Fiddles asked, and then said to me, "We've closed the old wing, for the moment," by way of apology. The old wing was herein distinguished from the new wing, which had been added to the house in 1820. "Once you're settled in, come to the conservatory for a little fruit of the barley tree. Inspector, I expect you'll want to confer with Hug... Constable Pennybun... I'll show you to the tower."

Canterfell Hall is formed of two wings wrapped lovingly around a remnant tower, the only earthly remains of the castle. Both wings are two stories high and in the Perpendicular Gothic style, so a lot of frightful gargoyles perched on top of vertical beams, looking down on one as though the whole affair is somehow one's fault. On the back of the new wing is the luxurious Blue Room, with an upper-floor view of the old wing and the tower to the left, and grounds to the right, set before a tastefully selected background of lake and forest.

Between the wings is a shallow reflecting pool, including a granite statue long since worn to a nub by the elements, depicting either George Slaying the Dragon or the Birth of Venus. The pool is fed by a man-made canal from the lake and formed of an egg-shaped depression in the lawn, lined with marble. This, in turn, is surrounded by flagstone decking, which at that particular moment was conspicuously decorated with a bold splash of Uncle Sebastian.

Following the trajectory upward, it was evident that the poor chap had been flung with some considerable force from the second floor of the tower. Had he achieved a slightly greater velocity he might have hit the water, any less and he'd have landed in the deep grass and, conceivably, survived.

I washed and changed for dinner or, rather, began to change for dinner, only to discover that my novel approach to packing for a weekend in the country had left me with four copies of the exact same thing — four cotton driving suits, four collared shirts, no spare undergarments at all, and only the tie I was wearing. I changed my shirt, for form's sake, and hastened to the conservatory.

The conservatory is formed of a wrought-iron pavilion in the French style, appended to the quiet end of the new wing. The ceiling and three walls are of glass, and the interior wall is composed of the rough stone of the exterior of the castle. The interior wall is host to a miscellaneous collection of eclectic artwork in eccentric frames. I found Fiddles alone, looking out at the garden with his hands behind his back and communing with a bumblebee which bounced rhythmically against the glass.

"Aren't you congenitally allergic to those things?" I asked.

"Oh, hello Anty," said Fiddles with a brooding, woe-is-me sort of inflexion. "Fatally, yes. It's why we can have no flowers in the house. Don't you think that's a monstrous pity?"

"On a scale of laryngitis to the Lusitania, I'd have to put it somewhere around no spare underwear," I said. "Talking of which, Fiddles, the fool who packed my bags for me overlooked some essentials. You couldn't see your way clear..."

"I'll have Vickers sort it," he said, somehow managing to make that, too, sound like something which weighed heavily on his artist's soul. "He's bringing the refreshments. I'll ask him then."

"Vickers?"

"The footman. We're having to make do. Lydde is the head of staff but I don't think he does much, leaving Vickers to manage cocktails and help at meals."

"Any relation to Rupert Vickers?" I asked. "My father's old valet was called Vickers."

"One and the same," said Fiddles.

"I rather think not," I said. "My Vickers was in his second dotage when my father inherited him from his father. He'd be a hundred now."

"Sounds about right," said Fiddles, and on cue the door opened and in stepped the bent and wizened form I'd last seen at my father's seeing-off, just under a year ago. He was the only one who shed a tear, if memory serves, and I and many others assumed it was because he was senile.

Vickers shuffled into the conservatory, relying on the drinks trolley for support.

"Shall I prepare the cocktails, sir?"

"Vickers," I exclaimed. "It's me, Boisjoly."

I saw my error, as the old eyes assumed a thick glaze of salty nostalgia.

"Mister Boisjoly," he said, his voice rising to the youthful timbre of a young man in his eighties. "It's a miracle."

"Ah, no, not as such," I said. "More in the line of an enormous coincidence. I'm Anthony, Vickers, son to Edmund Boisjoly, heir to the family fortune and unfortunate facial features."

"Young Master Anthony," said Vickers, with unconcealed disappointment. "Of course."

"Not even, any longer," I said. "I've reached the age of majority, if you'll recall, Vickers. It's just Mister Boisjoly, now."

"It's a pleasure to see you again, sir. How is your mother?"

"Tanned and tanked, last I heard," I said. "She left for the south of France immediately upon hammering down the headstone. How did you wind up here?"

"The conservatory, sir?"

"No, Vickers, Fray. How did you wind up at Canterfell Hall?"

Vickers assumed his full height, impressively, although I distinctly heard something crack. He was much more the butler than Lydde. His suit fit and his shoes shone, he wore white gloves and whiter spats. He looked at me beneath the subdued, hooded, reproachful brow I recalled from my youth.

"Canterfell Hall?" he said.

"Grandpapa shanghaied Vickers after your mother closed down the house in Kensington, isn't that right Vickers?" said Fiddles, helpfully.

"Ah, yes, Canterfell Hall," said Vickers, with mild surmise. "Shall I prepare the cocktails?"

"I'll manage, Vickers," said Fiddles. "Could you cannibalise my wardrobe and put together a care package for Mister Boisjoly?"

"Very good, sir," said Vickers. He arranged the decanter and syphon on the sideboard. "Most agreeable to have your company, Mister Boisjoly," he said, then turned, spotted the door, and employed it with great aplomb.

"Rummy thing, that," I said.

"Not really. Several years ago, Uncle Sebastian took a scythe to the domestic staff. There was blood on the walls, metaphorically speaking. Those who hadn't been deemed non-essential followed those who had right out the door, in protest of the high-handed manner in which their colleagues had been treated, or just because they objected to the increased workload. We couldn't convince anyone to stay on, and we had a devil of a time finding new staff while news of the massacre still rang across the land."

"While that is indeed rummy, it is not the rummy thing to which I refer, which is rummyer again by half," I said, sidling up to the sideboard beneath the reclining figure of Melpomene in a thin copper frame. Fiddles and I would often toast this muse of song and sorrow while drinking to double-vision in our youth.

"Which is?" Fiddles prepared two sloppy and generous whisky-sodas.

"Vickers is the footman? He was my father's valet. And before that he was his father's valet. I'd be unsurprised, in fact, if the legacy ran another three generations."

"I expect it's a matter of seniority," said Fiddles. "When Vickers joined the cast Lydde was head butler — only butler, in fact. It was his decision."

"He didn't strike me as a rounded professional," I observed.

"No, me neither, but when your house has a black cloud as ominous as that which Uncle Sebastian lobbed over Canterfell Hall you take what you can get."

"Talking of dear old Uncle Seb," I said. "I always held that to you he was merely old Uncle Seb. Frankly, I'm a little surprised to see his death has moved you so."

"What makes you think it has?"

"Come come, Fiddles. When I came into the room just now you were very clearly brooding on bees and, if memory serves, flowers."

"I don't know what you mean, old man."

"I mean, Fiddles, that it's unlike you to concern yourself with life's fancies. I vividly recall, when offered a rare private viewing of Uccelo's *A Hunt In the Forest*, you asking the rector what it would fetch at open auction."

"I still wonder about that."

"And yet I'm not here two minutes before you're making rash allegations about the local wildlife," I said. "If you're not mourning your uncle — and if I didn't know you to be a rank utilitarian with all the whimsy of a felled tree — I'd say that you were displaying the symptoms of having tripped head-over-teakettle for something with ruby lips and a native talent for twirling parasols."

"You know, you grow increasingly detached from reality in your declining years, Anty," said Fiddles. "Speaking frankly, it saddens me to see it."

"As you wish, Fiddles," I affected to concede. "Let's speak of happier things, then — what happened to Uncle Sebastian?"

"Ah, well, that's why you're here, Anty," said Fiddles. "Nobody knows."

"You knew this morning, Fiddles old man. He was thrown out a window."

"Exactly so," confirmed Fiddles. "The problem is that it's not possible. When last seen — alive, at any rate — he was in his study. Some time later a commotion is heard, shouting and whatnot, and then the unmistakable 'AAAAAaaaaaaa..... thack!' of an uncle falling from a great height."

"Doubtless a tremendous nuisance," I observed, "but hardly impossible. It's happened to better men."

"By a considerable margin, yes," agreed Fiddles. "But you know the study. It's on the second floor, back of the tower.

One door, one window, leading to a sheer drop. The tower was designed and built to resist the Norman hordes. The only way in or out is through the door."

"And?"

"And the door was locked, Anty, from the inside."

CHAPTER THREE
The Pertinence of the Improbable Parable

"Hug!" I exclaimed, on seeing my favourite copper in the den of the deceased.

"Mister Boisjoly." Hug stepped over a chaos of papers and sundry office supplies to shake my hand. "What a pleasure it is to see you again. It's been ten years, almost to the day, since I last took you in for creating a common nuisance in a public thoroughfare."

"I know. I'm sorry. What with one thing and another, time trips over itself. We must do it again very soon."

Hug was round and jocular, very much in the mould of the better country bobbies, or your Friars Tuck. He was perhaps slightly rounder and more accordingly jocular than when last viewed, but that only rendered the reunion like a Reuben forgery — more authentic than the real thing.

"Have you business here, Mister Boisjoly?" Ivor was standing at the open window, a notepad in his hand. I wandered casually into the room, hands in pockets.

"Not in any official capacity, no," I said. "How did you get this open?" I posed the question to Fiddles, and referred to the heavy oak door that stood twisted off its hinges. "It looks like it could stop a determined bull."

"Hug and I battered it down with that." Fiddles pointed to a small but heavy iron cannon from, at a guess, the 16th century.

"And the door opens inward, I take it," I said.

"It does, Mister Boisjoly," said Hug. "No chance of anyone tampering with the hinges."

"Very astute, Hug," I said.

"Mister Boisjoly, this is a murder investigation," said Ivor, making the state's case for the obvious. "I shall have to insist that you withdraw immediately."

"In a moment, Inspector," I said. "I note that the door has a two-way lock. Was there no other key?"

"Maybe," said Fiddles. "But it would have made little difference. The key was in the door on the inside."

I bent to examine the wreckage and saw that the key was indeed still in the lock.

"Could the killer have climbed to the roof after doing the deed?" I asked. "Perhaps with a block and tackle arrangement?"

Fiddles shook his head. "I was right outside the door. I heard the struggle. I tried to get in but, as I say, it was locked. When I heard him take the express route to the garden, I ran to the roof to have a look."

"And you'd have seen the killer on the stairs."

"Or on the roof, yes."

"Very good, Mister Boisjoly," chorused Ivor with his now familiar refrain. "I'll handle it from here. Mister Canterfell, why were you outside the door?"

"Vickers sought my assistance. He was bringing Uncle Sebastian his elevenses and heard a scuffle. He came to get me in the conservatory."

"And Vickers accompanied you back up the stairs?" asked Ivor.

"Vickers? Have you seen Vickers, Inspector?" asked Fiddles.

"No, why?"

"He's about a hundred and two," said Fiddles. "He had a sit-down in the conservatory."

"Returning to the roof, if you please, Fiddles," I said. "What did you see?"

"Uncle Sebastian with his head bashed in."

"And then what did you do?"

"I went back downstairs and sent Lydde to fetch Hug."

"Most wise," I said. "But during that time the door was left unattended."

"Briefly," said Fiddles. "But the tower wasn't. I met Lydde on the stairs, coming up, and sent him back down. And in any case, it's not as if the door could have become *more* locked from the inside."

"I see," I said. "And how long was it before Hug returned? Put more succinctly, how much time passed between the demise of Uncle Sebastian and the opening of the door?"

"That's it," said Ivor. "Constable, escort Mister Boisjoly to his room."

But Hug had taken out his notebook and I knew from experience that, like the blade of the ancient samurai, once the notebook was deployed it must needs be employed. "The time of death was approximately eleven fifteen," he said. "And I arrived at half-past twelve."

"By bicycle, Hug?" I queried. "Shouldn't be more than fifteen minutes from the station to here."

"I was, at the time that Mister Lydde come a-looking for me," said Hug, once again referring to his notes, "at the home of one Mrs Bede, clearing her gutters."

"Ah, that makes more sense. Carry on, Hug, what happened then?"

"I determined that the subject was deceased," said Hug.

"The urgency was somewhat passed at that point," said Fiddles. "We tried to break down the door. Couldn't do it. Then I recalled that I'd seen this cannon on the roof, so we went to get it."

"Who's we?"

"Hug and myself."

"Very resourceful, Fiddles," I said. "But again, the door was left unattended?"

"Lydde remained in place."

"Excellent. So," I tallied, "an hour and a half until Hug arrives, plus, what? Fifteen minutes to break down the door?" Hug and Fiddles nodded with synchronous certitude.

"And this was the state of the study when you broke down the door?" I said, rhetorically. We looked about us. The office was a study in studies, as it were. A simple oak professor's desk, a wooden swivelling chair with caster wheels, and a visitor's chair that appeared to have been selected for its extravagant lack of comfort. The walls were simple and solid but for the window and door. The window was in the French style and as tall as one man and as wide as two — ideal for the chucking out of one of them.

And it was in chaos. Papers, pens, a blotter, a lamp, and an inkpot had been swept from the desk, and all the drawers had been pulled out. The few paintings that there were — all depictions of the castle at different points in its history — had been torn from the wall, and one of them was smashed. The rug, which appeared to have been glued to the floor, had been violently pulled up at one corner.

"What's underneath this floor?" I asked.

"Roughly two feet of solid stone," said Fiddles. "It's why the carpet's glued down — Uncle Sebastian thought it would reduce heating costs."

"And did it?"

"Too early to say, really," said Fiddles. "It was only done last week."

"What possible difference can that make, Mister Boisjoly?" exasperated Ivor.

"As it happens, I'm about to embark on some rather exhaustive redecorating at my flat in Mayfair," I answered. "Seems a sound idea."

"That's it. Thank you very much, Mister Boisjoly," said Ivor, without so much of a hint of genuine gratitude. "Thanks to you, we know that the study was sealed from the inside, we know that it remained so for an hour and forty-five minutes, and we know that there was a single witness, outside the door." Ivor waggled his pencil as he spoke and made no effort to write down any of these insights. "And all of these salient facts, Mister Boisjoly, we had ascertained before your arrival. Now will you please leave, before I have you arrested?"

An unsettling silence followed this outburst. Fiddles and I looked at each other. Hug focused on some distant plane on which, I fancy, he was invisible.

"I say, Fiddles," I said, breaking the vigil as a humanitarian gesture to poor Hug. "Do you recall Dottie and Jules?"

"You know what?" said Fiddles. "I do. What an uncanny thing — I was just thinking of them myself. Can't think of why."

"I'm sure you can Fiddles old man. Cast your mind back — you'll want to hear this, Inspector," I said to Ivor, as he prepared to make manifest one of those steam whistles used in factories to announce the end of a long work day. "Jules was a sous-chef in the kitchen, in its storied days of gallic greatness, and Dottie was the upstairs maid."

"Are these people still in the employ of Canterfell Hall?" asked Ivor.

"Sadly, no," I said. "I offer them not as suspects, but as a guiding anecdote, like the parable of The Pharisee and The Tax Collector."

"Very well, Mister Boisjoly. What about them?"

"The Pharisee and the tax collector, Inspector? Or Dottie and Jules?"

"Dottie and Jules," insisted Ivor, with the tone of a man upon whose deaf ears the morality of parables would surely fall.

"Quite," I confirmed. "They were in love, you see, which under normal circumstances would be cause for rejoicing and the reading of the banns, but Jules was promised to another, a young lady by the name of, help me out Fiddles, was it Michelle?"

"Micheline, I believe."

"Micheline, quite right. But Micheline was back home in Arromanches-les-bains, and in no position to defend her interests. Nevertheless, in spite of Dottie's home field advantage, she lacked the support of the fans. The kitchen staff, to a soul, were also from the Normandy region."

Ivor looked briefly like a man with an important announcement to make, but then instead crossed his arms in a convincing combination of resignation and menace.

"Obviously," I continued, "Dottie and Jules were compelled to conduct their affair in complete secrecy. They would meet in the below-stairs servants' hall and whisper mortifyingly purple sentiments to each other, and yearn together for the day when they could run off to London."

I waited, then, to allow for what dramatists call the pregnant pause.

"And what, Mister Boisjoly, is the moral of the parable of the sous-chef and the upstairs maid?" asked Ivor.

"Take a moment to reflect," I said, giving the man a sporting chance.

Finally, he raised his chin and lowered his eyelids and looked at me as though he recognised me from a poster in the police station.

"If their affair was in confidence," he asked. "How did you know about it?"

"Exactly," I said, only stopping short of snapping my fingers by an act of immense will. I directed the attention of the assembly to the corner of the room, left of the door, where stood a funnel at the top of a wide copper pipe. The pipe was bracketed to the wall and it disappeared into the floor.

"A speaking tube, Inspector," I explained. "It was installed many years ago when the tower was modernised. It connects the rooms of the tower to the below-stairs servants' hall."

"We would listen to them for hours, sometimes," reminisced Fiddles. "It was better than the wireless."

"The sound goes both ways, Inspector," I explained. "The downstairs staff could hardly have failed to hear something useful during the murder."

The first dinner gong was echoing through the halls even as I scurried back to the Blue Room, and so I was grateful that Vickers was already there. He was dutifully stocking the drawers of my dresser with socks and underclothes, and he'd already draped the wooden valet stand in a black mourning suit.

"Ah, Vickers," I said. "You've saved my life. I thought I was going to have to dine in my room."

Vickers turned from the dresser and looked at me as though I'd come through the door in a suit of armour, carrying my head under my arm.

"Boisjoly," I reminded him. "Anthony. Son of Edmond."

"Yes, of course, Mister Boisjoly," said Vickers. "How pleasant to see you again."

"The sentiment is heartily reciprocated, my dear Vickers," I said. "I have nothing but fond memories of you clapping me about the ear as a child."

"I never enjoyed doing it, sir," said Vickers, in a mournful baritone, "but you would persist in stealing your father's cigars. He thought that I was selling them below-stairs."

"Yes, I know. Sorry about that Vickers. One can be quite blind to the consequences of one's actions at that age. And of course, there are few means with which to lay one's hands on a decent cigar, at ten years old."

"I sympathise, sir."

"Vickers," I said, as he helped me into my dinner trousers. "Are you quite happy here at Canterfell Hall?"

"I was very gratified to find a position so quickly after the house was closed in Kensington, sir."

"Yes, I can imagine, but are you quite happy here? You're the footman."

"Head footman, sir."

"Technically true, Vickers, but you're the only footman," I pointed out. "What do you make of this Lydde chap?"

"Mister Lydde is head of household staff, sir." Vickers buttoned my braces and put them over my shoulders.

"Come come, Vickers, no sense playing at manners with me," I said. "You held me out the pantry window while I evacuated my entrails of half a bottle of my father's best Armagnac. We have a bond."

Vickers helped me into my waistcoat and I turned to face him while he knotted my tie into a trim butterfly.

"It's possible that Mister Lydde exaggerates his station, slightly," he said. "One might say that he abuses his privilege to make unreasonable demands on his subordinates."

"A bully, eh?" I said. "I dealt with plenty of those at Eton."

"Indeed, sir? Might one enquire how?" Vickers held the mourning coat as I slid into it.

"It's case-by-case. Depends on the individual bully. Take Sally Hudson-Birch. Used to blacken my eye first day back from holidays, so it would heal in time for games day, when the parents would visit."

"Sally, sir?"

"Spencer, actually. Spencer Hudson-Birch. Built like a wine barrel. I think he had some sort of growing disorder, like the Elephant Man, but less photogenic."

"And how did you deal with Mister Hudson-Birch, sir?"

"I gave him the nickname Sally," I said. "Started a rumour it was his real name, in fact. Remarkably effective. He won a prize at the end of term and his picture appeared in the paper with the caption 'Sally Hudson-Birch receives first prize for scripture knowledge'. I still have the clipping, somewhere."

"I don't believe such a strategy would be effective against Mister Lydde," said Vickers.

"Probably not, no," I agreed, meditatively. "No two bullies are alike, you see. Does Lydde have any passions? Peccadillos? Peculiarities worth mentioning?"

"He holds some very progressive views on class and society, sir."

"You don't mean..."

"Yes, sir."

"Chilling," I said. "A communist, right here in the bosom of English aristocracy."

"Indeed sir. He's quite outspoken on the matter, in fact."

"He is, is he?" I said. "Well, then, it can't really be used against him. Anything else? Does he go in for ladies' foundation garments? Anything like that?"

"He is an inveterate eavesdropper, sir," said Vickers, clearly struggling.

"Isn't listening at keyholes among the principal obligations of office of a head butler, Vickers?"

"By convention, sir, yes."

"Not much there, then, is there. Anything else?"

"Not to my certain knowledge, sir, no."

"Well, leave it with me, Vickers. Something's bound to come to me. On a point of lesser import, do I understand that you were having a breather in the conservatory when Sebastian Canterfell gave forth upon the yielding air?"

"Yes, sir," said Vickers. "I was somewhat winded after descending from the tower and finding Mister Fairfax in the conservatory."

"Why the conservatory? That's almost as far as you can go in this house. Wasn't there someone nearer?"

"There may have been, sir," said Vickers. "I selected the conservatory as the most likely place to find someone with a key to the study at that time of the morning."

"What about below-stairs?"

"If I may speak frankly, Mister Boisjoly, I'm still unused to the premises."

"You got lost. Quite understandable."

"No, not quite. But I felt it likely that I would have done, had I not selected the direct route."

"Very sage, Vickers," I said. "So, you were in the conservatory at the time of the incident. Did you see it?"

"I did, sir."

"Did you see the assailant, by any chance?"

"I'm afraid not. My eyes aren't what they used to be. However, my attention was drawn to the tower window just in time to see Mister Canterfell ejected from it."

"Drawn? How so?"

"Mister Canterfell, sir. He was very animated, and loudly ordering someone to leave him, just prior to falling."

"Ordering someone to leave, you say."

"Yes, sir. He seemed most insistent that whoever was with him should depart."

"And that, apparently, is just what he did, but not before doing the deed and, somehow, leaving the door firmly locked from the inside."

"So I have been given to understand, sir," confirmed Vickers. "Most perplexing."

"This is the *mot juste*, Vickers," I said. "What's more, prior to departure the unknown assassin thoroughly searched the study."

"Indeed, sir?"

"Apparently. Any idea what he might have been looking for?"

"I'm not acquainted with the family's private affairs, Mister Boisjoly," said Vickers. "I can only think of the obvious."

"Which is?"

"The codicil, sir."

CHAPTER FOUR
The Main Course Mystery

When I finally came down to dinner, all the other residents of Canterfell Hall were gathered in the drawing-room, practicing their reproachful looks. Fiddles was by the credenza, playing bartender to a striking young lady in full flapper finery, including an ostrich feather in her turban the size of the jib-sail of a ship of the line. She was pretty and smiling and statuesque the way they like them these days in Hollywood, but she lowered an eyebrow on taking notice of me as though sizing me up through an unseen monocle.

Laetitia, the grieving widow, was in the corner with Hal, the grieving son, and the look they shot me gave me pause to wonder if I'd forgotten to wash some blood off my hands. Laetitia was dutifully packaged in black velvet which set an appropriately sober tone, contrasting with a generous decolletage and a string of pearls long enough to plumb its depths and come back up the other side.

Hal, like his cousin and, for that matter, I, was dressed in a midnight mourning suit, complete with tails, and all of us looked like we'd borrowed it. In my case I had done, and the jacket gave around the shoulders and waist to a degree that gave me the bearing of one whose years in a German POW camp still burned fresh in the mind. Fiddles was of a unique, eclectic architecture that made him the scourge of London tailors, and no matter how he was dressed, from academic robes to cricket whites, one was constantly tempted to remind him that he'd forgotten to remove the hanger. Hal's suit may have been finely tuned to his skeletal frame, but it would have been a wasted effort. He had a way of leaning into his clothes, as though relying on them for support. He would always tilt away, in a manner which seemed to defy physics, and hold his hands in readiness to knot his fingers nervously on a moment's notice. His voice was nasal and would be annoying, if it weren't already too busy being absurd.

Only the major, family patriarch and father of the departed, appeared unmoved by my arrival. He stood aloof and solid as a load-bearing column, pinioned on a spine that had been professionally ossified by years in the British overseas army. His aged face, that which could be seen of it behind a moustache like a foxtail stole, was a pastiche of emotion ranging from insouciance to indifference. He, too, was dressed in black coat and tails, but he was always dressed in black coat and tails, and he wore the crimson sash of His Majesty's Light Dragoons.

"Anty," called Fiddles with perhaps a soupçon more bonhomie than was called for, in light of the day's events. "Have a drink. Come and meet Rosalind. You remember everyone, I take it?"

"Please accept my most sincere condolences, Mrs Canterfell," I said with a subtle bow to the widow. She squinted at me across the rim of a long-stemmed martini glass, as though aiming it at me.

"What ho, Hal," I said. "Sorry about your father. Dreadful business."

"Hullo Anty. Thanks very, you know. Cheers, I mean," said Hal, with the same vaguely sycophantic stutter that I recalled from school. "How's your mother?"

Hal was two years behind us and so it was exigent upon us to abuse him mercilessly, establishing a lifelong dynamic. I suppose to him I was still the worldly upperclassmen, forever armed with a loaded ice bucket and convenient second-floor window giving onto the quadrangle.

"You remember Anthony Boisjoly, Grandpapa," claimed Fiddles, reflexively turning up the volume as one does when addressing a bushy grey moustache. The major had been taking my measure during the exchange with Laetitia and Hal, and he looked at me now with that same, scornful eye that had spoken "Why aren't you in uniform, young man?" for as long as I could remember.

"Beaujolais?" said the major, scandalised.

"Boisjoly," I corrected. "In the English form, of course."

"Ah, that's all right then." The major inspected me with the critical eye of one who knows a well-polished brass button when he sees one. "Knew a Boisjoly in Mysore. Commanded a unit of Sepoys in Bangalore. Any relation?"

"It's quite possible," I said. "We Boisjolys have left our stamp far and wide across the empire. Good soldier was he?"

"Frightful drunk," said the major. "Shot a horse during the king's birthday parade."

"Definitely a relation then," I said. "That's just the sort of stamp we tend to leave. My condolences about your son."

"Had a good innings," said the major, with that stoicism for which the British imperial soldier is so universally admired.

"Have a drink, Anty," said Fiddles, holding up a glass of golden icebreaker. "This is Rosalind. Rosalind, Anthony

Boisjoly." Fiddles gazed at Rosalind with the vacant smile with which little girls look at puppies, which went some distance in explaining his earlier practice of mooning over bees and flowers.

"Pleasure," I said, taking the glass in one hand and Rosalind's in the other. "Does Rosalind come complete with a family name?"

"Pierpoint," she replied, with a sing-songy sort of rhythm and a slightly higher register than I normally take my informal conversation, but otherwise charming.

"You're American," I observed.

Rosalind took on the demeanour of a young forest doe, suddenly and without warning asked to give its views on the Treaty of Rome. Then she said all that I needed to know about Rosalind Pierpoint.

"I know."

"Rosalind is of the Maine Pierpoints," said Fiddles. "She's Aunt Lettie's cousin."

"That's evident," I said, glancing back at Laetitia, a woman of robust figure, dark features, green eyes, and crow-black hair with a striking stroke of silver. Rosalind was fine-featured and petite, with wavy blonde hair and sky-blue eyes. "The resemblance is uncanny. You look enough alike to be close friends or acquaintances."

"Do you think so?" said Rosalind, squinting at Laetitia. "We're only distant cousins, *twice removed*. I didn't even know I had relations in England until I got a letter from a solicitor in Fray."

"Fray has a solicitor?" I said, amazed. "The bobby has a bicycle, and I noticed on the way here that the post office had been painted. Next thing you know they'll be digging a well. I suppose you can't hold back the inexorable march of progress."

"I expect it'll bog down a bit, though, after today," said Fiddles.

"Indeed, Fiddles?" I said. "Is today the start of some holiday of which I'm unaware?"

"No. Well, possibly, I don't know," struggled Fiddles. "I'm referring to Uncle Sebastian's plans for Fray. He was in the midst of negotiations with some London development firm. They were going to buy up everything between here and the inn."

"The entire forest?" I said.

"Just the bit between here and the inn, but yes."

"Why? Are they in need of wood?"

"Land, actually," said Fiddles. "They're short enough of the stuff to make Uncle Sebastian a firm offer. They were going to break ground during the summer. I expect that's off, now, or at any rate substantially nobbled."

"Does the inspector know of this?" I asked. "Where is he, anyway?"

"Doubtless he'll discover it in due course. He seems quite keen on the whole murder theme. He and Hug are dealing with the, uh..." Fiddles cast a brotherly glance at Rosalind and struggled for a euphemism for 'cadaver' before settling on "...the leftovers."

"I believe that 'remains' is the word for which you so bravely labour, Fiddles," I said.

"Wait a moment," said Rosalind. "Who's Fiddles?"

"Fiddles is Fiddles," I said, gesturing to my old college chum, Fiddles. "Fiddles, Rosalind. Rosalind, Fiddles."

"I thought your name was Fairfax."

"In fact it's Evelyn," I pointed out, helpfully.

"Evelyn?" said Rosalind, with that half smile that Americans use to indicate that if you're kidding, they're onto you.

"Perfectly respectable name," I said.

"In America Evelyn is a girl's name."

"Of course," I observed. "Yours is a country of immigrants. You have a greater supply of Christian names on which to draw. British resources are limited, and we have to ration carefully. For instance, the name Evelyn is shared by at least three people in this very room."

Rosalind replied once again with a fully armoured smile.

"It's true," confirmed Fiddles. "Hal and I go by our middle names, because our first name is Evelyn, and we're both named in honour of the major, Evelyn Clarence Canterfell."

"How adorable," enthused Rosalind, as though to suddenly find herself surrounded by Evelyns was as it would be for any other girl to find herself surrounded by kittens.

"It is," I agreed. "Adorable and admirable, honouring the old gentleman who has dedicated his life to serving his country, and amassing an immense fortune in the eastern fringes of the empire, most of which is bequeathed on his passing to those members of his family named in his honour."

"And that's just you and Cousin Harold?" said Rosalind, with a glance at Hal, who was in that instant choking on an olive.

"Cousin Harold twice removed," specified Fiddles, "So you and I aren't related at all. Like King Edward and Mary." Fiddles expressed this passing thought with a subtlety that stopped just short of dropping to one knee and offering Rosalind the ring which belonged to his mother.

"Talking of birthrights and bequests," I said, tilting discreetly toward Fiddles, "what's all this about a codicil?"

Fiddles' eyebrows rose with promise of lurid detail, but at that moment the doors to the dining room burst open and Lydde stepped into the drawing-room.

"Dinner is served," he said, with an intonation that, combined with what I now knew of the man, made the announcement sound like he was inviting us to pick the flesh from the bones of the working class. We filed into the dining room.

Vickers served at table, supervised by Lydde, who just managed to pour the wine. The trays were carried in and removed by a slip of a maid with the face and bearing of a sparrow. I gathered from Lydde's frequent recriminations that the sparrow's name was Luna, and that she had a nervous disposition.

The day had been long and trying, and I hadn't eaten since lunch. I never eat on or near trains, and I was very nearly regretting having had whisky-soda for tea. In short, I was well primed for the shameless abundance and exacting standards of the country kitchen in general, and the famous Canterfell generosity in particular. First warning that I was on a high-speed collision course with disappointment was the distinct odour of boiled meat, like soup stock simmering on a low heat for days, extracting the marrow from a rooster that had died of a broken heart.

Comparatively speaking, however, I do the aroma a disservice. Vickers gave us each a misshapen morsel of scalded flesh of unknown origin, and paired it with some vegetation which doubtless had once been green and innocent. Much debate ensued with regards to the pedigree of the meat. The major claimed the prerogative with the suggestion that it was mutton. Laetitia agreed, but on the condition that the major accept that it was a shank cut. Fiddles felt sure that we'd been served wild hare, but only because he'd spotted one earlier on the road that had been trampled by a horse. Hal's vote was for the horse and

Rosalind proposed that it wasn't meat at all, but some sort of construction material. As a guest, I naturally demurred from speculating aloud, but the taste and texture reminded me that I should have my riding boots resoled.

Dessert was therefore no surprise. It appeared to have been an apple crumble, but with the apple replaced by some more crumble. The wine flowed well, on the major's insistence, and it was the highlight of the meal. I normally pride myself on my talent for identifying the lineage of a grape, but this vintage was a stubborn mystery. I suspect it was a Spanish utility wine, used primarily to fuel heated political discourse in tradesman's cafés in Andalucia. It was a round, friendly bouquet, but otherwise largely incognito. It was bottled the previous year, obviously, after six to eight months in oak, and it was clearly a Merlot from the Ebro Delta, almost certainly the northern bank. Beyond that, though, I was utterly defeated. It could have come from any of three vineyards. Possibly four.

Dinner concluded with cheese and biscuits, and there was much rejoicing.

After dinner, the ladies left us to do whatever it is that ladies do after dinner. The major, too, preferred his own company, and made a conspicuous point of taking the whisky decanter with him. Fiddles, Hal and I were left alone with the port.

"Have you spoken to the inspector yet, Hal?" I asked, as Fiddles distributed generous overpours of a young, syrupy vintage, with hints of cherry and undertones of dull headache.

"We've been introduced," said Hal with a nod.

"I'm sure it was an epiphany for all concerned," I said. "But I meant with regards to the day's unfortunate events."

"He seems a terribly busy man."

"Frightens you, does he Hal?"

"Only a little," Hal said with a shrug. "Rather gives the impression that one is imposing on his time."

"I noticed that," I concurred. "Still, he'll want to know where you were when your father cast off the yoke of mortality."

"Doubtless. I had a rather exceptional view."

"Dubious pleasure," I observed. "Where were you?"

"The terrace sun room." By this Hal meant the high French doors on the ground floor of the tower. The quietest, brightest place in the house at that time of day, but it was designed with mathematical precision to look directly onto the centre of the reflecting pool, face-to-face with the statue of either Saint George or Venus.

"What were you doing?" I asked.

"Reading, but as luck would have it I looked up at the precise moment that Father connected with a flagstone."

"Are you quite sure that it was luck, Hal?" I asked. "Might your attention have been drawn by a noise? Shouting, for instance?"

"Not that I recall, but I confess much of what has occurred today has been, for me, quite novel," said Hal, thoughtfully. "It's quite possible that I've forgotten certain details."

"Quite understandable," I said. "What did you do then?"

"I went looking for Mummy."

"You weren't tempted to see if there was anything you could do for your father?"

"Have you ever seen a pumpkin dropped onto cobblestones from a second-floor window?" asked Hal.

"Of course."

"There was nothing I could do for him," said Hal. "I didn't want Mummy seeing Father in that state."

"Anty was asking about the codicil," said Fiddles, steering the conversation onto gentler paths.

"You didn't mention it to Grandpapa, I hope," said Hal.

"I didn't, no," I said. "But out of curiosity, would that have been a misstep?"

"Not as such, no," said Hal. "But you'd have been playing nicely into the old man's sadistic hands."

"No one knows, really, how the rumours of a codicil came about," explained Fiddles. "But the major takes insidious pleasure in neither confirming nor denying its existence. One prefers to not bring it up in conversation, for the same reason one tries to steer clear of any mention of the Siege of Malakand."

"Is there some question of its existence?" I asked.

"Let us say there's a range of opinions," said Fiddles. "I think that it started as a joke."

"I think the word you're looking for is threat," corrected Hal.

"Ultimatum might be the more accurate word," conceded Fiddles. "But it's irrelevant, because that's as far as it got."

"Oh, of course it exists," insisted Hal. "You don't know the old man like I do, living up in London all those years." Hal referred to the period between graduation and up until a year ago when Fiddles kept an apartment in Chelsea.

"What is the nature of this ultimatum, assuming it's not a mere whim?" I asked.

"The conditions of the will are broadly known," explained Fiddles. "Hal and I, both being equally Evelyn, split the lion's share of the family jewels, once the old man ceases to torment us. The codicil, ostensibly, amends it to further require that we serve in the military, and achieve an officer's rank before receiving our due."

I shuddered at the thought, and said a silent prayer of gratitude that my father hadn't been struck by a similarly mad flash of inspiration before his passing.

"Egads. No offence, gentlemen, but the prospect of either of you commanding His Majesty's cannon fodder in furtherance of the interests of the empire fails almost entirely to swell the proud English heart."

"None taken, old man," assured Fiddles. "And it's unlikely we'd be in command, in any case. They don't just make everyone officers, these days."

"But you're absurdly wealthy. And Canterfells," I objected.

"That sort of favouritism is reserved for the gentry, and their direct offspring," said Hal.

"You mean you'd actually have to earn an officer's rank?" I said, aghast. "Is that even possible, in an army of equals?"

"Presumably," said Fiddles. "I expect you have to save the life of a lesser royal, or slay a dragon or something."

"Or just be an earl," I observed.

"Or a duke. Or even a baron," mused Hal.

"Which is why I say there's no such thing as the Canterfell codicil," said Fiddles. "The old man's very big on family. It's why he's so keen on his direct descendants carrying on the name of Evelyn Canterfell. He'd hardly want that same family blood sinking into the sands of Waziristan. More port?"

"I won't, actually," I said. "I'm still working on this one. It appears to be stuck to the sides of the glass."

Fiddles looked at the decanter with a critical eye. "I know. Vile, isn't it? Part of Uncle Sebastian's cutbacks. I noticed that you managed to struggle through dinner without comment."

"I credit the illusion of artistic redistribution," I said. "I hid most of the boiled roofing tile under the purée of lawn clippings. I assume that the reputation of the Canterfell kitchen, once renowned throughout the land, is another victim of belt-tightening?"

Fiddles nodded, with his eyes closed, as one confirming one of the sad truisms of existentialism. "Dorothea Lively," he said, as though pronouncing the name of the fifth horseman of the apocalypse. "Not a poisoner by trade, in the literal sense, but a very talented amateur."

"Why do you keep her on?" I asked.

"Best we can do, actually," said Hal. "You remember that Cooper woman, Fairfax? Made tonight's disaster taste like ambrosia, by comparison."

"She'd often forget to make anything at all," confirmed Fiddles. "Or refuse to, out of protest at the absence of accolades from the previous attempt to murder us all with salmonella."

"Can't you get another French chef? Or one of those chaps who sell jellied eels around Aldgate Pump?"

"Not for what Uncle Sebastian was prepared to pay," said Fiddles.

"My father was only trying to see to it that something remained of the inheritance," contended Hal.

"This is disturbing news," I said. "I thought the Canterfell fortune was one of the kingdom's self-perpetuating resources, like the national strategic reserve of hedgehogs."

"I thought so, too," said Fiddles. "But I confess it was very much Uncle Sebastian's jurisdiction. I was only aware of the castle, the village, the Lloyds account returning some fifty thousand a year, the houses in Kensington, the apartment in Lambeth and the manor on Cap Ferrat, two hundred thousand in India bonds, and some ten thousand shares of the Bengal Savings and Loan. Oh, and we have a stable in Berkshire, with two winners last year at Epsom."

"So, at least a thin layer of protection against the vicissitudes of a booming, peacetime economy," I said.

"My personal view is that Uncle Sebastian just objected to barnacles on the hull, so to speak," said Fiddles. "He was always waylaying staff and pretending to not recognise them, asking them who they were and what they were doing here."

"Subtle," I observed.

"And of course that attitude extended to the village, in triplicate."

"I don't follow, old man."

"Most of the village is technically an extension of the castle grounds," he explained. "Much of it returns a substantial rental income, particularly the farmland. But Fray Wood, of which the villagers have free use for whatever it is that woods are good for — fishing and the mass murder of wild game, I expect — are run at what Uncle Sebastian considered a loss."

"Are woods expected to turn a profit?" I asked.

"While they remain woods, no, not really," explained Fiddles. "Which is why Uncle Sebastian was selling them off."

"Any indications of how the village is reacting to the news?" I asked.

"Not yet," said Fiddles. "The deal was only made public last week."

CHAPTER FIVE
The Lofty Window of the Loaded Widow

We dispersed after the port to rinse out our mouths, after which we were expected in the conservatory. I got no further than the drawing-room, where I found Rosalind on her own, playing something appalling on the piano.

"I can say with some confidence that I've never heard that instrument played so beautifully," I said.

"It's out of tune," said Rosalind, plucking a disconsolate note somewhere between middle C and a teaspoon scraping the bottom of a china cup.

"I know," I said. "No one ever plays it. They're not really a musical family, the Canterfells. I've known Fiddles to strike a wrong note on a dinner gong."

"Have you known him long?"

"Two ages, now," I said. "The child and the man. We were at Eton together, and then Oxford. We didn't actually begin the process of drifting apart until we moved back to London with our degrees, bachelorhoods, and dangerously bloated monthly stipends."

"What happened in London?"

"Choice of club," I said. "It can drive a wedge between the dearest of friends and make lifelong companions of mortal enemies."

"It's very kind of you to come down here at a moment's notice, then."

"We were at school together," I reminded her. "One doesn't just ignore an old school chum with a locked room mystery. Perhaps if we'd been to Cambridge, or it had been a simple case of poisoning, I might have been compelled to check my calendar first, but we went to Oxford. And what brings you to Fray?"

"I'm a keen photographer," she said, stroking a finger of dust from F sharp in the scale of G. "I'm capturing England."

"You're capturing England from Fray?" I said. "I fear that you risk letting the vast majority of the country get away Scot free."

"Oh, I don't know. I've seen rather a lot in the three weeks I've been here. Do you get many people thrown from windows up in London?"

"Do we? It gets so bad in the summer you have to avoid all major thoroughfares, or at least carry an umbrella. You didn't actually see Uncle Sebastian's maiden flight, did you?"

Rosalind shook her head. "No. Harold told me about it."

"When was that?"

"I'm not sure," she said, looking skyward for inspiration. "This morning, anyway. Initially, he just told me to stay away from the back garden, and wanted to leave it at that."

"But you didn't."

"No," she said with a disappointed sigh. "I thought he was hiding a surprise, so I made him tell me what happened. He would only say that something terrible had happened to his father, and he was looking for his mother."

"Did you know where she was?"

"No." Rosalind shook her head. "He left me to find her. Then that man Lydde came into the drawing-room. Is he very English?"

"Of a certain strain," I said. "Why?"

"He just makes me think of a hillbilly cousin."

"Do you have any hillbilly cousins?"

"No," she said, meditatively, "but if I did I expect they'd be like Mister Lydde."

"Without fully understanding the reference, I'm going to agree with that assessment. What did he say?"

"Nothing, really, I told him that something had happened to Sebastian, and he went to the tower."

"Ah, that fits nicely," I said. "Fiddles mentioned that he encountered Lydde on the stairs, on his way up. Then what did you do?"

"Went to my room," she said.

"Ah," I said.

"Yes," agreed Rosalind solemnly, which makes sense when one knows that the guest rooms are at the back of the new wing and the permanent rooms are at the front. This means Rosalind's room, like mine, afforded an excellent view of the contents of Sebastian Canterfell's cranium.

"I'm sorry you had to see that," I sympathised.

"Me too. I was glad to have not eaten breakfast."

"There was no breakfast served this morning?"

"There was, but it smelled a little like a gasworks. And it looked quite a bit like a cowpat."

"Kidneys, would be my guess," I said. "A delicacy in this country, when prepared right. You were wise to avoid it. Has Fiddles been much comfort?"

"Comfort?" asked Rosalind. "In what sense, comfort?"

I was aware of a sense of danger as I proceeded, as though I'd turned down a well-known and well-travelled street in Mayfair and discovered myself on a frozen lake.

"In the sense of, well, comfort. Of the emotional, platonic, vaguely avuncular variety. Comfort," I said, as one taking a turn in a spelling bee that had become nasty in the elimination rounds.

"Why should Fairfax be comforting?"

I felt like the unprepared explorer, having set out across the unforgiving desert, and finding himself unsure if safety lies in turning back and attempting a return journey for which he's certain he has insufficient water, or forging ahead into the unknown. Anyone who knows me even passingly well would be able to tell you which I chose.

"I caught the poor sap in the conservatory this evening, ruminating unmistakingly over bees and flowers."

"What's that to do with comfort?"

"Almost nothing," I conceded, "but it concerns you a great deal indeed. Fiddles is intolerant of bees and he loathes flowers, likely because bees do not. And yet, there he was, lamenting the cosmic injustice that was the absence of posies on the premises."

"I think you left out the part that has anything to do with me," Rosalind helpfully pointed out.

"Do you mean to tell me you haven't noticed that when Fiddles looks at you he takes on the speech, demeanour and facial expression of one who's been hit on the back of the head with a cricket bat?"

"Is Fairfax not always like that?"

"On the contrary," I said. "On a day-to-day basis he's an explosively dull personality. Pragmatic to a fault. He read law at school, you know. I recall many an evening, over milky tea,

Fiddles complaining of the sibylline flightiness of the Patents Act of 1901."

"Fairfax wants to be a lawyer?" Rosalind posed the question as she might if she understood 'lawyer' to be synonymous with 'dogsnatcher'. I felt behoved to set the record straight.

"Parliamentarian," I said, straightening said record in a stroke. "Like his father before him, who currently occupies the formerly safe seat of Fray."

"Formerly?"

"Very formerly, by all accounts," I said. "Halliwell Canterfell, the Fairfax's father in question, has been tremendously entertaining in parliament, but for all the wrong reasons, and in a manner which has not translated into popular support at home."

"What does that mean for Fairfax?"

"It means that, contrary to one of the proudest traditions of British democracy, Fiddles will not automatically inherit his father's seat in parliament, once Halliwell retires to a life of persecuting the ducks, or whatever it is these country gentlemen get up to."

"That's very unfortunate," said Rosalind, with a tone that suggested that she may be aware of those who have endured greater hardship in life.

"For Fiddles it is," I contended. "It's been his childhood dream to contribute to the affairs of state. He has very strong views on free trade with the Americas, and the governance of hedgerows."

"I'd hate to see him disappointed."

"As would I. I've only ever seen him show any passion about two things, discounting a brief flirtation with the Charleston. I hope I'm not the bearer of bad news."

"No," said Rosalind, meditatively. "No, Fairfax is cute. I like him. It's just... I didn't come to England for romance."

"Well, you probably didn't come here for murder, either," I pointed out. "We have to be prepared for life's little surprises."

Pursuing a by now obsessive thirst, I accompanied Rosalind to the new wing and as far as her room, where I deposited her on my way to the conservatory and the promise of a richly-deserved whisky and, to a lesser degree, soda. The inspector had let it be known that he expected us to assemble there after dinner, but only Laetitia had arrived. She was standing at the sideboard, contemplating the reclining figure of Melpomene. The sun had long since set, and the night made mirrors of the glass walls and ceiling. I availed myself of the decanter and syphon.

"May I compose you something irresponsible, Mrs Canterfell?" I offered.

"Thank you, Mister Boisjoly," she said, with the unmistakable crackle of a proud woman who has been drinking steadily and alone, and thinks it doesn't show. "But as you can see, I have one already." She held up, to illustrate the point, an empty glass.

"Perhaps I could refresh it for you," I offered.

"Maybe just a little one," she acquiesced.

I topped up her drink, leaving little room for idle debate of the whisky-to-soda ratio question.

"So, how are you holding up?" I asked. "Anything a vacuous young bachelor with little to no life experience can offer in terms of comfort and support?"

Her shoulders shimmied, slightly, as a woman floating on

gentle waves, and she selected one of my eyes and looked hard into it.

"What are you doing here, Mister Boisjoly?" she asked.

"Oh, you know, getting a bit of country living in. Fresh air, sunshine, chaps thrown out of second-story windows. London can get so stifling in the summer, don't you know. Fiddles — your nephew Fairfax — asked me down."

"I thought you might be a friend of my son's," she said, with undisguised relief.

"Well, we're hardly sworn enemies, but Hal was behind us at school. And he was the more high-minded — always going in for poetry appreciation and which Frenchman painted this or that interpretation of *Le Déjeuner sur l'herbe*, while we were out rowing on or falling into the Thames, depending on the time of day."

"He's a very sensitive boy," said Laetitia, seemingly with a view to presenting the observation as some sort of defence.

"Oh, indeed, and all the better for it," I hastened to assure her. "I'm among those who are only too grateful to those willing to brave the unforgiving frontlines of poetry appreciation, so that others might not."

Laetitia raised her chin and assumed an imperious air, or as imperious an air as she could manage in her condition. The effect was more a combination of autocratic and slightly miffed at something.

"He's a very sensitive boy," she said, putting the sentiment to a pleasant tune that rendered it as though hearing it for the very first time. "So unlike his father."

"Oh?" I said, not wishing to speak ill of the dead, but not above soliciting a bit of salacious gossip, either. "Was Mister Canterfell not of a sympathetic nature?"

Laetitia made a sort of "pish" sound, like she'd sprung a

sudden leak, and said, "The man was a coldwater fish."

"Doubtless one of the more affable varieties, though, surely. Halibut, say."

"Why exactly did my nephew invite you, Mister Boisjoly?"

"I have something of a reputation as a problem-solver among my social circle in London," I said, swirling my drink in a manner contrived to convey modesty.

"Is there a problem that requires solving?"

"Well, your husband's passing does bear some of the hallmarks of a mystery," I said.

"How so?"

"Who killed him, for one, and how, for another."

"I thought he was thrown out a window." Laetitia walked to the glass and would have been looking out on the scene of the crime were the windows not reflective against the night.

"Did Hal not tell you what happened?"

"He didn't need to," said Laetitia. "I saw it."

"Oh, I see," I said. "Might I ask how?"

"I was in my room."

"Your bedroom?"

"That is typically what is implied by the term, Mister Boisjoly."

"I see," I said, the way one says things one does not mean at all. "It's just that I thought that the permanent rooms were at the front of the house."

Laetitia regarded me as I imagine Russian chess masters look across the board at an opponent who's fallen neatly into the Lasker Trap. "I refer to the Chartreuse Room, where I often sleep. My husband and I did not always find it convenient to share a bedroom."

The Chartreuse Room, like my own Blue Room, looks directly out onto the carnage.

"Most disturbing," I said. "I'm sorry you had to see it."

"I didn't see much. I heard the scream and when I looked out the window it was over."

"That's it? Just a scream?"

"Followed by a bit of a dull thud. Like someone hammering in a fencepost."

"Vivid. Then what did you do?"

"I went looking for Harold."

"Did you find him?"

"Not straight away, no," she said, with an inebriated calm. "Lydde told us that Harold was already aware of what had happened to his father."

"Us?"

"I encountered the major in the main hall. He had been in the gallery."

The gallery is what the family affectionately called the major's museum of keepsakes on the first floor of the tower. Its window, like that of the study above it, looks out on the back garden.

"Then the major saw it too," I said. "How very disturbing for the poor man."

"He's seen worse."

"So I'm reliably informed by the horse's mouth," I said. "Did you proceed to the study?"

"The drawing-room," said Laetitia. "Lydde told us that he was on his way to fetch the constable. I thought it best for us to wait in a room with no view of the back garden."

"Most wise," I said. "You must be a great comfort to your father-in-law."

"The major is in no need of comfort, least of all from me."

"Of course," I said. "Tell me, has he ever mentioned anything to you about a codicil?"

Laetitia repeated her uncanny air leak imitation. "Take my advice and don't ever ask him about that damned codicil."

"I'll add it to my collection," I said. "Hal and Fiddles offered me the same sage counsel. They, however, can't agree if it even exists."

"Oh, it exists alright," assured Laetitia.

"You seem quite sure," I said. "Have you seen it?"

"No, but it would be just like the major." She drained the remains of her drink, somehow adding a note of resignation to the comment.

"Any idea what it says?" I asked.

"The major is very big on blood relations," she said. "My guess is that it adds some criteria to his will that excludes anyone who isn't his direct descendant."

"Such as, for example, your good self?"

"This is the first example that leaps to mind, yes," she confirmed.

"Doesn't the current will leave almost everything to Hal and Fiddles, the two Evelyns?"

"You don't think that's a little peculiar for a will?"

"Not very, no. He loves his grandsons and wants to know they're taken care of."

"Of course," said Laetitia. She placed her glass on the sideboard in a very deliberate fashion. "So why not just mention them by name?"

"Doesn't it?" I created another unbalanced blend, granting shameless favouritism to the whisky over the soda.

"Not exactly. The whole point of the will is to encourage a proliferation of Evelyn Canterfells. Any descendants so named enjoy an equal share of the estate."

"In that instance, I wish to amend my original judgement," I said. "It is a little peculiar. It doesn't explain the codicil, though."

"The will is witnessed, and kept on file with the family solicitor," said Laetitia. "It can't be a secret. The whole point of the codicil is that nobody knows what it says, so the major can enjoy his last great pleasure in life — watching his family jump through hoops."

At that moment the door opened and our bubbling soirée doubled in size and energy with the injection of Constable Hug and Inspector Ivor. Hug had about him the jocular quality of the boy scout about to perform or having recently performed a good deed. This appeared to leave little good humour to be shared among the forces for law and order, obliging Ivor to scowl gravely, as one carrying the weight of the world on his shoulders.

"What are you doing here, Mister Boisjoly?" asked the inspector, the moment he laid eyes on me.

"This is the question on everyone's lips," I said. "Mrs Canterfell was just asking the same thing."

"I requested that the members of the Canterfell family gather in the conservatory, Mister Boisjoly," said Ivor. "Are you a member of the Canterfell family?"

"In the closest possible sense of the term," I said. "Fiddles and I rowed together at college."

What would doubtless have been an eloquent tribute to the eternal bonds formed by school athletics was cut short when the aforementioned entered the room.

"Hello Fiddles," I said. "Drink?"

"I will, thanks."

"Inspector? Hug?"

"Not while on duty, thanks, Mister Boisjoly," said Hug, as

though turning down a whisky-soda in sacrifice to the obligations of uniform was a rare honour, and he didn't know when he'd next get the chance.

Hal and the major entered next. The major was recounting one of his many adventures in the east, and Hal was repeating a cordial "uh-huh, uh-huh" as I myself have done on similar occasions.

Finally, Rosalind entered, and I was getting dangerously close to running out of whisky. Thankfully, Lydde arrived a moment later with the refill trolley, with Vickers in tow to perform the actual refilling.

"I realise it's late, and you've all had a trying day," announced Ivor, with the staccato delivery of a man lighting his pipe. "But I'm going to crave your indulgence just a little while longer. I'm going to need everyone to wait outside this room. We'll start with you, Mister Canterfell." He addressed this to Fiddles. "And then, one at a time, I'll ask you to return to the conservatory to make a statement regarding your disposition and what you may have seen or heard at the time of the unfortunate incident and no, Mister Boisjoly, this does not apply to you. You're welcome to return to your room or, ideally, to London."

"I was going to ask if this also concerned the household staff," I said, lowering the hand which I had been waving like a schoolboy with a head swimming with declensions.

"The staff has already been interviewed."

"I see," I said. "I'm most curious to know what was heard from the downstairs end of the speaking tube."

Ivor, too, appeared stirred by the prospect, and he smiled slightly before saying, "Nothing, Mister Boisjoly. Thank you for your input, but not a sound was heard through the speaking tube."

"But surely someone was well within listening distance of the device at that time of morning," I said.

"Mister Lydde and Miss Lively, the cook, were both in the servants' hall at the time."

I regarded Lydde with an authoritative eye. "And you heard nothing?"

"Not a sound, sir," he confirmed.

"We'll try not to take up much more of your time," continued the inspector, with a smug sort of delivery, as though my lob had just been declared 'out', "and we'll leave the search until the morning."

"Search?" Fiddles spoke the word that was on the tip of every tongue.

"Immediately following the murder, the killer searched Mister Sebastian Canterfell's study thoroughly," explained the inspector. "It stands to reason that whatever he was looking for is key to the killer's motive."

"But doesn't it also stand to reason that whatever it is, he's got it?" asked Fiddles.

"On the contrary," said the inspector. "The search of the office was thorough, and it grew in intensity as it progressed. This suggests that the killer was frustrated in his efforts. He even pulled up the carpet. In short, he searched everywhere, a contingency which would have been unnecessary had he found whatever it was he was looking for."

"So you propose searching the house, Inspector?" said Hal, with reasoned incredulity. "Do you have any idea how big this house is?"

"The killer expected to find it in the study," said the inspector. "In fact, he was so sure that he'd find it there, he murdered Mister Canterfell before setting about looking for it. I conclude that whatever it is, it is not far from the study, and is hidden in a manner much like that which the killer thought it would be. We shall begin with the tower, and proceed methodically to the new wing."

"You're going to search our rooms?" asked Rosalind, expressing a lady's preserve for the intimacy of the boudoir.

"I regret the intrusion, madame," said the inspector, with the timbre of the professional who makes few distinctions between lady's preserves and a hole in the ground. "But yes. Furthermore, you will all be asked to restrict your movements between now and tomorrow, when the search is complete. Constable Pennybun will be on the premises to remind you of this request, if necessary. Lydde?"

"Yes?" said Lydde, who leaned against the door frame, ready to spring into action.

"Where do you normally serve breakfast?"

"In the drawing-room, sir."

"Not tomorrow. Until further notice the common area of the house is off-limits. You can serve breakfast in here," said the inspector with finality.

"I object to this... incarceration," said Laetitia, slowing somewhat as she approached the second syllable but rallying nicely on the fourth. "Are we suspects?"

"Yes, madame," said the inspector. "With the unfortunate exception of Mister Boisjoly, everyone in this house is considered a suspect in the murder of Sebastian Canterfell."

CHAPTER SIX
The Mystery of the Missing Muse

Breakfast was a jolly affair. The morning sun was concentrated by the glass walls and ceiling of the conservatory, giving one the novel impression of dining at the interior of an electric light bulb. There were no dining facilities in the conservatory, apart from the sideboard, which Vickers and Luna, the maid, were cluttering with a considerable improvement over last night's fare. Four shallow but voluminous brass trays presented, in order of importance, crispy bacon and smoky kippers, runny fried eggs, black blood pudding, racks of hard toast, and great, clay pitchers of lemon squash, clinking with ice and dripping condensation. It was all unexpectedly excellent, and I took the issue up with Fiddles.

"This comes as something of a relief," I said. "Has your Miss Lively experienced some sort of spiritual awakening?"

"In a manner of speaking," said Fiddles. "Breakfast is typically like this, if not better. Yesterday we had kidneys."

"You don't say. With something of the aroma of a gasworks about them?"

"Just so," confirmed Fiddles. "Utterly divine."

We were compelled to dine garden-party style, with plates balanced on our knees and teacups on the floor. The entire household turned out in varying degrees of mental competence after a trying day and well-irrigated evening. Laetitia, in particular, had the air of one standing gamely at the prow of a ship as it was rocked by an angry sea. The major ate heartily, standing up, and Rosalind appeared to be one of those rare girls to whom the morning shows all lenience that is within its scope to bestow. She was distant, though, and in particular appeared to navigate the conservatory in a manner explicitly devised to avoid collision with Fiddles. Conversely, Fiddles was in fine humour, and appeared to have forgotten that Rosalind Peirpoint had ever been born.

Hal was in a whimsical mood, and he ate his kippers alone, on the chessboard, seated by the garden and looking up at the tower. The formality of the previous evening was part of the murky past, and everyone was dressed for a fine summer's day, with the exception of the major, who appeared to be dressed to deliver the commencement address at a military academy.

I took a plate of his favourite things to Hug, who was stationed outside the door of the conservatory.

"Here you are, Hug," I said, passing him the plate. "Kippers and bacon, and some more bacon, just like many fondly remembered *lendemains* in the cells."

"Most considerate, Mister Boisjoly," said Hug, taking charge of the plate like a penitent receiving communion.

"Tell me Hug," I asked, reluctantly, because there's no sight that more rewards silent contemplation than that of an Englishman enjoying a kipper, "did you pass an eventful night?"

"Nothing of note, Mister Boisjoly."

"How disappointing," I said. "Not your fault, of course, but I was hoping that there'd been suspicious manoeuvres in the darkness. No covert whispers? Creaking hinges? The dull tumble of a heavy body dragged across an attic floor?"

"I suppose there could have been," said Hug, comfortingly. "I was in the conservatory most of the night."

"Stretched out on the divan, did you? I don't blame you. It's dashed comfortable, that divan; small but close and clubby, like the couchette to Milan. Have you ever taken the night train to Milan, Hug?"

I made a quick mental note to myself to get to the bottom of Hug's experiences with transcontinental trains at a later date, because at that moment a piercing scream did what piercing screams are designed for, and Hug and I were drawn back into the conservatory.

The entire Canterfell collection was gathered around Laetitia, who was glaring wide-eyed and wider-mouthed at a space on the wall just above the sideboard. All eyes followed hers and saw at once what had stirred her so.

"My painting," she said, with a depth of emotion that overvalued a depiction of the reclining nude of Melpomene by, to my mind, roughly a hundred thousand pounds.

Nevertheless, the facts of the matter were essentially correct — the painting was gone. This was not, on its own, a development of particular significance, and certainly not warranting a gaping of the mouth and the extending of a trembling finger, as Laetitia was now doing like a haunted figure in a poem by Poe. No, the gravity of the missing painting was found in the fact that, moments earlier, it wasn't.

We had all seen it. I'd seen it, certainly, and while none of us actually checked in that morning with a committed, "I observe that the painting of Melpomene is on the wall, where it always is," it stands to reason that had it not been there it, enquiries would have been made.

"Is there a painting gone missing?" asked Hug.

"An oil of the muse Melpomene," I explained. "Of the Manet school, I'd say."

Hal laughed heartily at this, as I might have expected him to, had I remembered that he was there.

"Manet?" he said, with a childlike joy. "I hardly think so. If you'd said Renoir, even as a blind guess, I might credit it, but Manet?"

"So, this Renoir bloke painted it," deduced Hug. "Was it very valuable?"

"Renoir didn't paint it," said Hal. "No one knows who painted it, nor do we know its value."

"It was a cherished gift," said Laetitia, who had recovered her composure and gathered it into a state of high dudgeon.

"When did you last see it?" asked Hug, drawing his notepad and pencil with the methodical deliberation of the master of masonry, drawing hammer and chisel.

"Not five minutes ago," said Laetitia.

Hug looked around the room, then with clear-eyed perception said what everyone was thinking.

"Then where's it gone?"

Now we all looked about the room and determined that, at a cursory glance, at least, the painting was nowhere to be seen.

"Did anyone see where it went?" asked Hug, drilling down to the core of the matter, as an experienced police officer will.

"It couldn't have gone anywhere," said Fiddles. "It was definitely there at breakfast — I toasted Melpomene with my lemon squash. Just now, when I returned to the sideboard for more bacon, I noticed it was gone."

"Who screamed, then?" asked Hug.

"That was I," said Laetitia. "When Fairfax pointed out the outrage, I couldn't contain myself."

"Very understandable," I said. "Few things are more unsettling than the pilfering of a cherished muse."

"Did anyone leave the room since you last saw the painting, Mister Canterfell?" Hug asked Fiddles.

"No," said Fiddles. "And in any case, Hug, weren't you in the hall?"

"Someone might have gone into the garden," said Hug in swift defence.

"Nobody left," said Fiddles. "We're all here."

"I'll ask you all to remain where you are," said Hug, "while I institute a search."

"Good morning, Constable." All attention turned to the door and the arrival of Ivor.

"Inspector," said Hug. "There's been a robbery."

Ivor responded with a withering look. He appeared in that moment distinctly like the sort of man who preferred his larceny in the later afternoons.

"Good morning, Inspector," I hailed. "Did you sleep well? The Hare's Foot is famous for its soft beds and landlord's own best bitter, which is said to have a sedative effect. My personal experience is entirely the opposite, in the main, and I'm very curious to have your views."

"I cannot recommend the inn, I'm afraid," said Ivor. "The landlord, Mister Porter, is a dangerously curious man, and I was harassed at dinner by a local eccentric, who persecuted me with his insane views on the exclusive claim of the descendants of Edmund Ironside to the British crown. Now, what's this about a robbery?"

"The painting, sir," said Hug, indicating an obvious gap on a wall otherwise festooned with paintings, etchings, prints, and a cameo commemorating the summer that Princess Helena spent at the castle in 1863, with a view to putting an end to an undesirable match with a German archivist.

"What's become of it?" asked Ivor, with a tone conveying the weight he accorded a painting gone missing during a murder investigation.

"It's disappeared, sir," said Hug. "But no one's been in or out of the room."

Ivor paced some distance from the sideboard. He stood looking at it and lighting his pipe. Then he reapproached.

"It's fallen behind the sideboard," he announced, and a flurry of activity ensued.

"Nothing," said Hug, astounded that the inspector had missed the pocket.

"Roughly how large is this painting?" asked Ivor.

"So big," said Laetitia, describing a rectangle of about shoulder-width with her hands.

Ivor smoked his pipe and regarded us all with the squint of the professional cynic.

"It's been rolled up," he announced. "Or folded, and one of you is hiding it on his person. I'm afraid that you'll need to be searched."

"Inspector," I said. "Are you familiar with the case of Vincenzo Perruggia?"

Ivor looked at me the way a side looks at a thorn.

"You might know him better by his work — in 1911 he stole the Mona Lisa from the Louvre Museum in Paris, right under the noses of staff and security."

"Very well," said Ivor, by way of conceding that what I had to say may have been pertinent to the case at hand.

"Signor Perruggia, ostensibly motivated by national pride and a desire to return *La Gioconda* to her homeland, walked into the Louvre, dressed like an employee, and walked out again with the painting."

"How?"

"Exactly, Inspector," I said. "How did Mister Perruggia do it? It was initially concluded by the police, just as you have done, that he removed the painting from its frame, rolled up the canvas, and hid it under his clothes."

"I presume you're about to tell me otherwise."

"Very prescient, Inspector," I said. "I am. The Mona Lisa, which prior to the theft was merely recognised as one of many works by Leonardo Da Vinci, by the way, has one very rare thing in common with the missing painting of the reclining nude of Melpomene."

"Which is?" Ivor removed the pipe from his mouth and crossed his arms in an articulate "Get on with it" gesture.

"They're both painted on wood, Inspector."

Ivor looked to Laetitia for confirmation, but got it from Hal.

"It's true, Inspector. It's painted on a thin but solid sheet of hardwood."

Ivor looked upon Hal as a valued informant from that moment on, or perhaps more accurately as a valued alternative to myself.

"Could anything have been hidden behind this painting, Mister Canterfell?"

Hal looked for inspiration at the gap in the gallery wall. "I doubt it very much, Inspector. I've had it down once or twice. It's got backing paper to the frame, of course, on which is written a cryptic inscription, but it leaves no space for any hidden documents."

"Nevertheless," said Ivor. "It's evident to me that an impossible murder and an impossible art theft on the same premises within twenty-four hours are very much related."

Vickers and Luna reappeared at that moment with the tried-and-found-true tension breaker, tea. The sideboard was transformed from breakfast nook to tea station with a thrill and a flourish and a balancing act which gave me new respect for the slip of a maid. We gathered around the tea tray, now beneath a rectangle of wallpaper in the original cornflower yellow, the rest having been faded by years of summer sun without benefit of the protection of Melpomene.

"How long had it been there?" asked Ivor.

"Seventeen years," said Laetitia, in a distant sort of way, as though she'd only just that moment realised that seventeen years is a longish bit of time.

"Right, Constable?" said Ivor, with the tone of one inaugurating official proceedings. "We'll begin our search here, and then move to the rest of the new wing, so that those wishing to leave the conservatory can do so as soon as possible."

"You don't mean to suggest that we're confined here," protested Laetitia.

"I mean to suggest nothing of the sort, Mrs Canterfell," said Ivor, telegraphing his punchline. "Instead you may regard it as official police instruction during a murder enquiry." And there it was. "At the risk of labouring the obvious, I'll point out that it must have been someone in this room who spirited off your painting."

Hug and Ivor looked behind the remaining paintings on the only wall which wasn't made of glass, and had then exhausted all possible recesses in which something could be hidden in the conservatory. Then they left us, presumably to rifle the paintings and private papers in our rooms.

Even the consumption of tea, normally a source of endless amusement, grew tiresome, and when the major had the inspiration to escape to the garden I followed along.

"Lovely morning, Major," I said, shouldering up next to him as he gazed in the general direction of the lake. I doubtless would have characterised the morning as lovely, as a matter of form, had it been raining hot stones, but it was in fact an objectively lovely morning. The grasses, neglected by goat and groundskeeper, waved a synonymous English green at us in a lush halo around the reflective blue pond, formed of a swell in the river, from which it meandered drunkenly through the estate before stumbling into the forest and becoming hopelessly lost. The sky was an unblemished sheet of cyan, iridescent behind a shimmering yellow sun that appeared to have positioned itself directly above Canterfell Hall. The splendour of it all gave voice to a chorus of birds, each of whom sang with the abandon that can only be achieved when murder is foreign to your entire species.

The major looked at me with the charming absence of familiarity that they train into all British soldiers, starting from the rank of lieutenant. By the time a man has achieved the level of major he can look into his own dear mother's dying eyes without a hint of recognition.

"Boisjoly, isn't it?"

"It is," I confirmed. "Of the Bangalore, horse-maiming Boisjolys. I understand that you were in the gallery during yesterday's unfortunate occurrence."

The major nodded curtly. "I was returning my arrowhead."

"Your arrowhead, sir?"

"My arrowhead," he repeated. "You're surprised to

discover that I have an arrowhead?"

"On the contrary, Major, I'm surprised that you have just the one."

"Took it to the leg in Mandalay."

"Ah yes, of course. I recall you telling us about it. I thought it was a bullet, though."

"You're thinking of the Khyber Pass," said the major. "Right buttock."

"Oh, I see," I said.

"What do you mean by that, young man?"

"In fact, Major, I'm not sure that I mean anything at all. It just seems the safe thing to say when talk turns to bullets and buttocks."

"I was facing the enemy, if you must know. I was shot by an overzealous Punjabi."

"Terrible bother, zealousness," I said, sympathetically. "I avoid it religiously. Tell me, Major, why did your arrowhead need putting back? Had it gone missing?"

"It was on loan to The British Empire Exhibition. Got it back last week."

"The British Empire Exhibition?" I said. "What a tremendous honour."

"You'd have thought so," said the major. "But nevertheless they sent it back."

"Ah," I said, deftly avoiding another 'I see'. "And while you were in the gallery, did you hear anything unusual?"

"If you regard the screams of a dying man unusual."

"I do, in fact. Was that all you heard?"

"It was enough," said the major. "I looked out at the garden and saw Sebastian in that undignified state."

"Terrible way to go."

"I've seen worse."

"I daresay you have."

"Once saw a man being eaten alive by a tiger."

"Good Lord," I exclaimed. "What did you do?"

"Shot him, of course."

"The tiger?"

"The man. It was too late for him. Doubt he'd have wanted to go on in that condition, even if he could."

"No, indeed."

"Still have the rifle, if you're interested in long-range firearms."

"They're among my greatest passions, Major," I said. "In fact I'd very much like the opportunity to familiarise myself again with your gallery of adventures."

"Can't just now," said the major. "That inspector fellow is searching the castle."

"Just so," I agreed. "What do you suppose he's looking for?"

"Damned if I know."

"You don't suppose it's your codicil, do you?"

I don't know what sort of reaction I was expecting from the old man, but that which I got was most curious — he smiled, longingly, as though inwardly recalling the memory of some sweet mischief.

"I doubt that very much," he said.

"It just occurs to me that it would be most helpful if the inspector were to know the actual location of the codicil, don't you think?"

"Doubtless it would," agreed the major. "But I regret that I don't know where it is."

"How unfortunate," I said, and together we continued to silently contemplate the scenery. I clasped my hands at my back, and gazed toward the horizon, and then again gave voice to inspiration. "Nevertheless, it might be useful to at least know the contents of the document. Do you think you could at least see your way clear to sharing the general gist of the thing? Not with me, obviously, but with Inspector Wittersham?"

"I fear not," said the major, with a deliberate stoicism that struck me as excessively cold-blooded, though perhaps not among the sort of men who shoot other men as they're being eaten by tigers.

I continued to clasp my hands at my back and brood on the middlefield, the universal sign for inoffensive amenability. Finally yet another inspiration came to me, this time with a quiet certainty.

"You've forgotten whether or not you wrote a codicil, haven't you Major?"

"I have," he said, with a sober acceptance of his diminished capacity that did him credit.

CHAPTER SEVEN
The Affair of the Abayant Earldom

It was a little over an hour before Hug returned to deliver us from captivity.

"Turn anything up, Hug?" I asked as the others hurried to their rooms.

"I'm not at liberty to say, I'm afraid, Mister Boisjoly," said Hug.

"Really?" I said. "And where did you find it?"

"In the bedroom of Mister Canterfell," said Hug, before mentally slamming on the brakes and reversing. "I mean to say, I'm not at liberty to say, Mister Boisjoly."

"And you haven't done, Hug. You've discharged your duty to the highest standards of your office. There are three Mister Canterfells on the premises, and that's not counting the dead one and the one in London."

"The inspector was quite specific, Mister Boisjoly."

"Of course, Hug, think nothing of it," I said, much to Hug's evident relief. "Have you seen Vickers in your travels?"

"I expect he's below-stairs."

"Handily, that's exactly where I was about to go," I said and did just that.

Below-stairs is only actually below the stairs at the front and back of the house. On the side of the new wing, it gives onto the garden where it slopes away to the river. This is what serves as the tradesman's entrance at Canterfell Hall, and the drunken student's entrance in the summertime of our youth. The stairs from the dining room lead to the servants' hall — the theatre in which played so many riveting episodes of the Tragic Romance of Dottie and Jules. This leads in turn to the kitchen — the scene of the many triumphs of the Canterfell table when it was French — and from there to the aforementioned tradesman's entrance.

Vickers was in the below-stairs hall, polishing silver.

"Hello Vickers," I said.

It had been some hours since Vickers had last seen me, and consequently he had entirely forgotten who I was. I allowed him a moment to come to the light on his own which, after a few moments of productive blinking, he did.

"Mister Boisjoly," he said. "Is there anything wrong?"

"Not at all, Vickers," I assured him. "There's nothing unusual about a below-stairs Boisjoly. We're a democratic clan, by instinct. And at any rate, I have urgent business with that speaking tube." I gestured to the copper pipe which descended from the ceiling and came to a stop at ear level, where it presented a funnel. "Is it still operational, to the best of your knowledge?"

"It's not commonly employed in the house, sir."

"Why not?" I asked. "It's hours of fun."

"It only connects to the tower, sir, directly above us. There's only the study and the gallery."

"What if the major takes a sudden fancy for a bowl of

porridge while he's playing with his tin soldiers?"

"An unlikely contingency, sir. The major is rarely in the gallery, and only Mister Sebastian made use of the study. He was a man of strict routine. He would occasionally use the speaking tube to give instructions for elevenses, but otherwise come down for meals."

"What about yesterday?"

"He used the device to ask that I bring him tea at eleven o'clock."

"Interesting," I said. "And what time was this?"

"Just after breakfast, I believe. Approximately nine o'clock."

"So it was certainly working yesterday," I concluded. "I suppose I'd better have a look, nevertheless."

I put my ear to the funnel. Nothing. Not even the unique sound that nothing makes, when heard through a tube, or described as the sound of the sea, when heard through a conch shell.

"Curious," I said. "Can I borrow one of those forks, Vickers?"

Vickers passed me a fork and I pushed it into the darkness of the funnel and as far up the tube as it would go before being blocked by something suspiciously yielding. I pushed a bit harder, and then withdrew the fork. On the end of it was a good-sized baking potato.

"There is a tuber in this tube," I said to Vickers. "Is that some downstairs practice of which I, handicapped by privilege, am unaware?"

"Not to my knowledge, sir. It may be a custom unique to Sussex," said Vickers, with broad-minded forbearance.

"You know what I think, Vickers?" I said.

"I wouldn't presume, sir."

"I think that someone deliberately blocked this speaking tube."

"It does seem an improbable situation to come about by chance."

"Just so, Vickers," I said. "Rather a lot of improbable things appear to occur at Canterfell Hall, wouldn't you say?"

"It's not for me to comment, sir."

"Take that painting that went missing from the conservatory, right under everyone's noses."

"Painting, sir?"

"Painting, Vickers. Specifically of Melpomene, initially the muse of song, suddenly and without cause demoted to the department of tragedy. Do you know it?"

"Only distantly, sir, thanks to a brief exposure to the classics when I was a boy."

"I'm unsurprised. You've always struck me as one to hide his intellectual light under a bushel," I said. "But I was referring to the painting, about yay big..." I held my hands up, indicating a rectangle the size of a 'yay', whatever that may be. "...with a simple copper frame."

"I believe I do know the painting, sir." Vickers focused his full attention on a fish knife.

"I believe you do, too, Vickers," I said, then, stepping in closely and lowering my voice. "Where is it now?"

"I have not yet had occasion to remove it from the premises."

I looked to the shelf behind me, about shoulder height, on which were stacked a dozen brass serving trays.

"It's still with the rest of the trays?" I asked.

"I'm afraid so, sir."

"It's probably as good a place as any," I said. "It got it out of the conservatory, and there were two policemen in the room at the time."

"I cannot recall when I was more nonplussed."

"I'll bet," I said. "Still, you accounted for yourself admirably. One might have thought you were Vincenzo Perruggia himself."

"You're most kind, sir."

"I mean it, you were the very model of grace under pressure. I wish I could say the same for your accomplice."

"You deduced Mrs Canterfell's role as well, then, sir."

"Not until just this very second," I said. "But it had to be someone. You weren't in the room when she removed the painting from the wall and fitted it under the other trays. How did she organise it with you?"

"Mrs Canterfell asked me last night to remove the painting from the conservatory, but Constable Pennybun's presence rendered that impossible," said Vickers, absently massaging a soup tureen. "But when it turned up among the trays, I surmised what had happened."

"Crafty," I said. "Any idea why?"

"No, sir."

"You have an admirable sense of discretion, Vickers," I said. "I wish I shared it, but I don't. I'm going to have a look."

"I would prefer that you didn't, Mister Boisjoly," said Vickers, with the authority of a man with the winds of social convention at his back. "My first duty is to the household."

I folded my arms and leaned against the hall shelves, regarding Vickers in a new light. Or, rather, the old light, the one under which I viewed him when he could, with a disapproving glance, send me back upstairs to polish my shoes.

"Very well, Vickers," I said. "If you'll tell me this much, I'll forget that I know the location of the painting and how it got there — is there anything hidden in it? A codicil, for instance, affixed to the back?"

"Nothing like that, sir," said Vickers, visibly relieved. "There is a simple inscription, of a somewhat sophomoric quality."

"I hope you appreciate the restraint I'm exercising, Vickers," I said. "I have an abiding passion for sophomoric poetry. I used to practice the art myself, in my younger days, and once sent an oeuvre to Susan Royce-Phipps in which I compared her modesty to the peeking light of dawn."

"Your self-discipline does you credit, sir."

"So long as it's acknowledged."

"It is, sir."

"Now, back to the problem of the potato," I said, holding the vegetable up again on its fork. "Is the notorious Miss Lively in the kitchen?"

"I believe so, sir."

"Then I shall leave you, Vickers, with this piece of advice — in your future criminal endeavours, try to select your co-conspirators with greater diligence. It's imperative."

"I'll bear it in mind, sir."

"See that you do."

The kitchen was at the end of the hall and largely as I remembered it. It was a vast space, as spacious and as equipped as the kitchen of any hotel restaurant. The walls were white tiles, floor to ceiling, but for the tradesman's entrance, which was all door and window, so that the copper pots and pans suspended from the ceiling scintillated in the early afternoon sun. There was a decidedly provençal quality to the scene, seasoned with simmering pots on the stove, fresh produce on a worked and worn oak table, and a stack of forest firewood and the country scent of it burning in the oven. Luna, the maid, was at the table, slicing vegetables, and when I entered she started as though I'd intruded as she was chopping up a body. A short, stout woman that I took to be Dorothea Lively was at the broad stove — as big as any two, fully-grown stoves — staring into a cauldron as though it had just made a derogatory comment. In spite of their differences, she had much in common with the cauldron, and both were round and squat and showed signs of being overheated. Miss Lively was further adorned with grey hair, tied back in a messy bun, and thick black eyebrows.

"Miss Lively?" I said, and in an instant the woman forgot the offence given by the pot and turned a look of cold condemnation on me. I held up the potato.

"Do you recognise this?" I asked.

She squinted at the thing for a moment and then, satisfied with her analysis, announced, "It's a potato."

"Exactly, Miss Lively," I said. "It *is* a potato. Do you know if any of yours are missing?"

She looked at me with a grimace composed of knuckled brow and protruding lower lip.

"No?" I continued. "Very well, perhaps you could help me with this, then, was anyone in this kitchen yesterday morning who isn't here usually? This would have been between the clearing away of breakfast and when Vickers took tea up to the study."

"Of course not," said Miss Lively.

"Are you quite sure? It's rather important."

"I was here all day," she said, and then leaned forward, as though to share a confidence, and whispered, "preparing dinner."

"Yes, I was here for dinner last night," I said. "Hard to believe that took the entire day to prepare."

Her demeanour changed markedly at what she evidently received as a compliment. She smiled warmly, and then took my arm and led me to the stove.

"Want to know my secret?" she asked.

"Ptomaine?" I suggested. She shook her head, smiling enigmatically. Then she reached across the stove and seized a clay jug by the neck, as though it had been about to make a break for freedom.

"Sherry," she said, pulling the cork from the mouth of the jug. "It's good for everything." She trickled a modest taste into the cauldron with which she'd been quibbling, and gave it a stir with a big wooden spoon. She withdrew the spoon and held it up for me.

"Try that," she said, and I obliged. "What do you make of it?"

"I'm not sure," I said, reflecting. "I suppose it depends very much on what it's meant to be. Might be a passable consommé, or a quite unforgivable gravy."

"Needs more sherry," said Miss Lively, in agreement with some unspoken proposition. Then she swept the bottle to her lips and drank from it like it granted youth. She set the bottle aside and said, with a satisfied smile, "That's better."

"You're quite certain that you would have noticed if someone was here yesterday morning?" I asked.

"Absolutely," she confirmed. "Nothing gets past Dorothea Lively. Shall I tell you something, Mister...?"

"Boisjoly," I said. "I'm agog."

"Shall I tell you something, Mister Agog? I've worked in great houses since I was a girl."

"You don't say," I said.

"I do say. And if it's one thing I've learned, working in great houses, it's to keep mum about such things as I notice."

"Things, Miss Lively?" I said. "What sorts of things?"

"Take last night, for instance," she said, squaring up to fix my eye with a frank effort at focus. "No one finished their dinner. Every plate come back like it went out."

"Most disturbing," I said. "Doubtless appetites were affected by the unfortunate demise of Mister Sebastian."

"Oh, yes," she said, vaguely. "I'd forgotten about that."

"How about you, Luna?" I called across the room, causing the maid to throw a carrot over her shoulder in a spasm of surprise. "Did you see anyone in the kitchen or servants' hall yesterday morning?"

"Luna weren't here," answered Miss Lively on the maid's behalf. "She's got her upstairs duties in the morning."

Luna, relieved of the burden of social intercourse, bowed her head once more to her task.

"Mister Boisjoly?" My family name was mercilessly mangled from the kitchen door by Lydde. "Mister Canterfell, the one who's your mate, wants to see you in the conservatory."

"Thank you, Lydde," I said. "Goodbye for now, Miss Lively, Luna."

"Luna?" said Lydde, as though just noticing her. She shrank beneath his gaze. "You still down here? Beds don't make themselves, not in the houses of the bourgeoisie."

"Yes, Mister Lydde," said Luna, with an obsequiousness at which the meekest toady in the court of Louis XIV would have shaken a censorious head. She wiped her hands on her apron and scampered from the room.

Lydde crossed his arms and subjected Miss Lively to a malevolent smile.

"I trust you'll manage lunch without further encroaching on the duties of my staff," he said, and I made a mental note to inform Vickers that I had identified the strategy to be employed against this particular bully.

Whatever Lydde's flaws, his reporting of the facts was above reproach. Fiddles was in the conservatory, as promised, and he wanted to see me.

"Ah, Anty, there you are," he said. "Drink?" He began making music with the decanter and syphon.

"It's just gone noon, Fiddles."

"Has it?" he said, looking around for a clock and, finding none, elected to accept my word. "We'll make them singles, then."

"Lydde said that you wanted for company," I said, receiving a crystal tumbler.

"Rather," he confirmed. He stood tall with his drink and fixed me with a frank gaze. "Anty, I have a confession to make."

"Then by all means unburden your heart, old chum, and you may be assured of absolution."

He opened his mouth as though to speak but decided the light wasn't quite right. He walked to the glass wall and looked out at the garden.

"It's too late for absolution, old man," he said. And then continued with "What I want to confess is…" but whatever it was that Fiddles was about to reveal would have to wait, because in that instant Hug and Ivor appeared at the door.

"Mister Canterfell," interrupted Ivor. "I would like a word."

"Oh, hello, Inspector. Hug," said Fiddles. "Drink? It's only gone noon, so we're just having short ones."

"Mister Canterfell, a document has been found in your possession," said Ivor.

I looked at Hug, whose efforts to avoid my eye caused

him to look about the room as though hypnotised by a housefly.

"A document?" asked Fiddles. "What sort of document?"

Ivor held up a piece of paper. It had gravity, as paper goes. It appeared to be a letter, on quality stationery, with some sort of printed seal.

"Do you recognise this, sir?"

Fiddles looked at it from across the room, but appeared satisfied with what he saw from there.

"Ah," he said. "I can explain that, Inspector."

"I'm very glad to hear it," said Ivor. "Because I think you'll agree that it requires explaining."

"May I see that?" I asked.

"No," said Ivor, flatly. "Mister Canterfell?"

"It's a letter from the Committee of Privileges," Fiddles said for my benefit. "They're restoring our title."

"Title?" I said. "What title?"

"Oh, didn't I mention that, Anty? I felt sure that I told you about the Earldom of Fray."

"And yet I feel quite sure that you did not, Fiddles," I said. "Would you care to now?"

"Seems opportune, yes. We have an earldom. It's been in abeyance for about two hundred years."

"Abeyance?" said Hug.

"In suspension," explained Fiddles. "The title can only be inherited by male offspring, and some two hundred years ago the only remaining descendants of Anfeld Bunce, First Earl of Fray, were girls. In accordance with the law of the land, the title fell into abeyance."

"It's been all girls for two hundred years?" marvelled Hug.

"Well, no, there've been male descendants since then, but either they never petitioned the crown to restore the title, or they weren't qualified."

"What qualifies one to be an earl?" I asked. "Isn't it principally a matter of knowing when to wear ermine to church?"

"In the main, yes," said Fiddles. "But when I say qualified I mean a male descendant with a clear claim."

"And what makes a claim unclear?"

"Well, for instance, if two cousins were descendant via their mothers, then each would have an equal claim and so, in the eyes of the law, neither would be qualified."

"The major," I said.

"Exactly," confirmed Fiddles.

"The major?" Hug said, with a query in his voice corresponding to what he perceived as an unjustified change of subject.

"When the earldom is restored," explained Ivor. "The major will become the Fourth Earl of Fray, isn't that correct, Mister Canterfell?"

"Yes, I suppose so. Well-deserved recognition, wouldn't you say, gentlemen?" Fiddles raised his glass. "Here's to Major Lord Fray."

"Hear, hear," said Hug, with a spirit that started strong but faded in the absence of popular support.

"And since the death of Sebastian Canterfell," continued Ivor, "the next in line of succession is your father, followed by you."

"Yes, I suppose that's true," said Fiddles. "But this is the bit I meant to explain. When I made the petition, Hal had the clear claim to the title."

"Exactly, Mister Canterfell," said Ivor. "What you've described is a motive for murder."

CHAPTER EIGHT
The Puzzle of the Purloined Poison Pen

"Motive isn't everything, Inspector," I said.

"That's correct, Mister Boisjoly," said Ivor. "There's also opportunity, and Mister Canterfell was the only person in proximity of the study when the murder was committed."

"Apart from the murderer, of course," I added.

"Mister Canterfell went up the stairs, according to his own testimony and that of Mister Vickers," said Ivor. "Subsequently, Sebastian Canterfell was pushed to his death."

"Motive and opportunity aren't everything," I said. "There's also means, and so far we've only established that nobody, including Fiddles, had the means to force Sebastian Canterfell out his window."

"Mister Canterfell, you said that from outside the door, you heard your uncle calling out for the keys," said Ivor.

"That's correct," confirmed Fiddles.

"And that you called back to him, saying that the door was locked from the inside."

"Also correct," said Fiddles, assuming something of an attitude. "And true."

"Did you know that the major was in the gallery, one floor below, and that he claims to have heard nothing of the sort?"

Fiddles looked at me, his eyebrows calling out for support.

"Inspector," I said. "I don't think I'm divulging any family secrets when I say that the major struggles to remember certain details."

"That, and the peculiar nature of the crime, is why Mister Canterfell has not yet been charged," said Ivor, then to Fiddles he added, "But I would ask that you remain within the confines of the estate while the investigation continues."

Ivor turned on his heel and was gone. Hug smiled awkwardly, loitered even more awkwardly, and then he, too, was gone.

"So," I said to Fiddles. "You're going to be an earl."

"Assuming I don't hang for murdering my uncle, first."

"Either result is bound to create considerable social distance between us," I observed.

"I suppose it might, rather. You haven't had one of your insights yet, then."

"Not yet, old man, but it's just a matter of time," I said. "Unless you did it, of course. You didn't do it, did you?"

"No, I didn't," said Fiddles, without conviction. "Refresher?"

I handed him my glass and he turned it back into something worth holding onto.

"Does look dashed bad for you, though," I said, taking a seat on the close and clubby divan. "Why did you petition to restore the earldom if you stood no chance of claiming it?"

"Prestige, mainly." Fiddles sunk into a leather armchair across from me and balanced his drink idly on his knee. "I may face something of an uphill battle for the constituency seat, should my father ever retire from parliament. Nothing greases the gears of political machination like a noble in the family."

"But you can see how it looks. Now that your father is next in line after the major, he'll have incentive to quit parliament and go into the House of Lords."

"My father has no love for the House of Lords," said Fiddles. "He'd quit government altogether first."

"Do you somehow think that looks better for you, Fiddles?" I asked. "It amounts to the same thing, only sooner."

"Yes, I suppose that does look rather damning, doesn't it?"

"On a possibly related note, Fiddles," I said. "What was it that you were about to confess to me when the inspector interrupted?"

"I'm glad you asked that," Fiddles sat up and leaned into this new line of enquiry. He put his drink on the table between us, freeing up his hands to fidget independently. "What do you make of Rosalind?"

"Lovely girl."

"I know. Delightful. This is what I was about to confess — you were quite correct in your initial analysis of my state of mind, Anty, I'm absolutely dippy for her."

"Well, congratulations, Fiddles. It seems an ideal match, although yours is only one party in a decidedly two-party arrangement."

"Yes," said Fiddles, with a despondent look. He took up his drink and folded himself back into the recesses of the armchair. "This is the problem at hand. We've had a falling out."

"Of what nature?"

"I'm quite honestly not sure," said Fiddles. "Not really my strong suit, the fairer sex."

This was a statement of bald fact. Fiddles had always been of a famously pragmatic nature and known for drearily legalistic views on the subject of romance. Compelled to study the classics by Oxford's stubborn insistence on turning out well-rounded barristers and legislators, he once wrote in a paper that Ophelia would have been better advised to bring an action against Hamlet for breach of promise.

"Something must have sparked it. Did you say something in character? You didn't compare her beauty to a water-tight legal brief, did you?"

"No, nothing like that. In fact, I was being quite solicitous." He searched the ceiling for inspiration. "I'm aware of my limitations as regards the poetic, so I was expressing simple curiosity about her, asking her about her family, friends, interests, that sort of thing."

"You do rather have a way of presenting idle curiosity as an interrogation," I suggested. "But you worry needlessly, old chum; misunderstandings of this nature are the milestones on the road to true love. You just need to contrive another opportunity to find yourself alone with Rosalind, and apologise."

"Apologise?" said Fiddles. "How can I apologise when I don't know what I've done?"

"My dear Fiddles, you're not apologising for something you've done or said, you're apologising for upsetting Rosalind. You're expressing your regret at having given offence, for you regard your relationship with her as precious, and it wounds you deeply to know that you've jeopardised it with your enthusiasm for her charms."

"I say, you couldn't write that down for me, could you?"

"It's more a general idea, Fiddles," I said. "Keep the intention in mind when you talk to her and the words that come will be yours."

Fiddles found further depths in the chair into which to sink, and he was now almost horizontal. He balanced his drink on his chest and looked at me through it.

"I doubt I'll get the chance," said Fiddles. "You see, I was rather consumed, briefly but firmly, with the injustice of the thing. I didn't feel that the ticking off she gave me was quite commensurate with whatever crime I'd ostensibly committed."

"What have you done, Fiddles?"

"I'm afraid I've gone and written her a note," he said. "Giving back as good as I got, as it were."

"Fiddles you absolute brick," I said, much with love as admonition. "As a trained barrister you should know as well as anyone the perils of hot action."

"I know," said Fiddles, low woe in his voice. "I've never felt about a girl the way I feel about Rosalind, and my passion put a cudgel in her delicate hand."

"Pity you couldn't have been that poetic last night," I said.

"Or as I was in that letter," said Fiddles, looking into his glass. "I was quite eloquent, in my ire. I was particularly expansive on the subject of her accent, and the habit she has of saying 'hmm?' rather than 'I beg your pardon'."

"I suppose this explains the Siberian enmity I noticed between you two this morning."

"No, in fact, she hasn't seen the letter yet."

"Then for all intents and purposes, Fiddles, it doesn't exist. Destroy it, immediately, and erase its existence from your memory. Do you really need to be told this?"

"She hasn't seen it because it has yet to be delivered to her, but it's out of my hands," said Fiddles. "I put it with the post this morning."

"You mailed it to her? She lives here."

"I didn't mail it to her, no, I addressed it to her and put it with the post, so that Lydde would deliver it."

"And he has yet to do so?"

"I rather think that if he had she'd have quit the castle by now, her curses echoing in its halls for days," said Fiddles. "No, he mailed it."

"Why did he do that?"

"You'd have to ask him that," said Fiddles. "Frankly, I find the man somewhat intimidating. He told me that he took the outbound mail to the post office, and he said it in a manner that suggested that was all I was entitled to know."

"So, at some point, it's going to return to Canterfell Hall."

"Exactly," confirmed Fiddles. "Probably quite soon, in fact. It's not as though it needs to go far."

"And we need to intercept it," I surmised. "You were right to call upon me. I'll deal with the letter, you focus on working your way back into Rosalind's good graces."

"You don't think it's too late?" Fiddles said, looking at me as Robinson Crusoe is said to have gazed at sails on the horizon.

"Of course not," I assured him. "Assuming you're not arrested for murder."

As luck would have it, Luna was in my room when I got there, changing the bedding.

"I'm sorry sir," she said, endeavouring to hide behind a pillowcase. "I'll return later."

"Not at all," I said. "I've only come back to change my shoes. I'm afraid that I felt very much at risk of getting lost in those I borrowed from my host. And as it happens, I was hoping to confirm a couple of points with you. Have you spoken to the police?"

In lieu of a verbal response, she bit her lower lip and vibrated slightly. I took that as an affirmative.

"Can you recall where you were yesterday around eleven o'clock?"

This time she managed a rapid nod.

"You can? Excellent. We're really making progress now," I said. "Where would that have been?"

"I was below-stairs, sir, clearing up from breakfast."

"At eleven? Are you sure? That seems rather late to be clearing away the breakfast dishes."

"It weren't the dishes," she stammered. "I mean, it weren't breakfast. I mean, it weren't eleven."

"Luna," I said, with the voice I imagine I'll employ if ever asked to convince a suicidal nerve patient to abandon his place on a tenth story ledge. "It's none of my affair if clearing up after breakfast took longer than anticipated. In my view you do a sterling job in light of how short-staffed the castle is. I just need to know what you saw between nine and eleven yesterday morning."

"I didn't see anything, sir."

"Well, who was below-stairs with you?"

"Mister Lydde and Mister Vickers come in for the breakfast trays. I helped carry them up."

"And who was in the servants' hall at eleven o'clock?"

"I'm not sure, sir. Me. Mister Lydde."

"Excellent. And then what happened?"

"Mister Lydde went upstairs. I went to the laundry."

"At precisely eleven? Did you hear or see anything unusual?"

"I needed to get started on the bedding," she said. "There

was all the permanent rooms to be done, plus two guest rooms."

"Two guest rooms? Why two? I thought there was just Miss Pierpoint staying at the castle."

She looked down at her feet and watched them shuffle for a bit.

"Ah," I said. "Of course. That Boisjoly fellow. My apologies."

"No bother, sir."

"Nevertheless, I shall see to it that your excellent work is brought to the attention of your employer."

"You're very kind, sir."

"Luna!" Lydde appeared in the doorway, barking like sheepdog at a miscreant lamb. "I've been looking all over the castle for you."

"Why?" I asked.

"Eh?" said Lydde.

"Why were you looking all over the castle for the chambermaid, Lydde?" I asked. "Where else would she be but in the chambers? Where did you look first, I wonder, the coal cellar? The livery stable?"

"Are you endeavouring to tell me my business, Mister Boisjoly?" he asked, arms folded and chin jutting like a forward-mounted cannon.

"Clearly somebody needs to," I said. "If you regard searching for chambermaids in the messuages of the estate to be among them."

Lydde staggered, metaphorically, under the blow, and he reached for support in a most surprising place — he looked pleadingly at Luna. No man, least of all brittle egos like Lydde, likes to be embarrassed in front of a woman for whom he has tender feelings.

"Perhaps we should leave Luna to her work," I proposed, as a tacit mutual cessation of hostilities. "I was hoping to have a word with you, as it happens."

Lydde acquiesced and we walked together back toward the main hall. He evidently did not have any business with Luna, but was merely jealous of her company. My suspicions were confirmed.

"I understand that you were below-stairs when yesterday's events occurred," I said to him.

"That's right."

"Can you recall what happened after that?"

"I went upstairs, to do my rounds."

"Your rounds, Lydde?"

"The conservatory, the drawing-room, the terrace. The ruling class likes to be attended to, as I'm sure you know, Mister Boisjoly. I do rounds between meals, to see if anyone needs anything."

"But you didn't get a chance to do your rounds yesterday," I said.

"No, sir. Miss Pierpoint was in the drawing-room. She told me something had happened to Mister Sebastian, in the tower, so up I went."

"If I recall, the stairs to the tower, the entrance to the drawing-room, and the stairs to the new wing all depart from the main hall, is that still the case?" I asked.

"That's right."

"Did you encounter anyone else? The major, for instance? Or Mister Harold?"

"No, I didn't."

"And then you went to fetch the constable."

"I suppose someone had to do it."

"Very civic-minded of you, Lydde, it does you credit," I

said. "Talking of your duties, I wonder if you can advise me on another matter altogether — the post."

"The post, sir?"

"Just so, the post. I gather that you took some letters to the post office this morning. Is there any chance, if I were to make haste, that I could get them back before they were mixed in with the furious commerce in parcels that is the Fray postal service?"

"Not a chance," said Lydde. "I took the mail early this morning, before breakfast."

"How unfortunate. Why so early?"

"I was taking an urgent telegram to be sent to London."

"To whom?"

"Can't you ask Mister Canterfell that?" asked Lydde, rather turning the tide in the battle of convention.

"I suppose I could," I confessed. "To which Mister Canterfell do we refer?"

"Mister Harold, sir," said Lydde, and this admission released a torrent of confession. "It was to his Uncle Halliwell, informing him of the death of Mister Sebastian."

"But I received my telegram yesterday," I pointed out. "Couldn't you have sent the telegram to his honourable member for Fray at the same time?"

"No, sir, I couldn't, for the very good reason that there weren't no telegram to Mister Halliwell yesterday. Two trips to the post office is the same as one, when you're born into the class that don't have to make no trips to the post office."

"Very well, Lydde," I said. "Would you do something for me, then, and let me be the first to know when the afternoon post arrives?"

I released Lydde to continue on his merry way, for I would be alone to consider this new development. Fiddles hadn't sent a telegram to inform his own father about the death of his uncle, the aforementioned own father's own brother.

CHAPTER NINE

The Conundrum of the Confrontation on the Khyber Pass

As I stood in the upper hall of the new wing, the major brushed past at a brisk canter.

"Ah, Major," I said. "How fortuitous. Are you heading to the gallery by any chance?"

"Eh?" The major stopped and looked at me from a vantage point somewhere about the top of his nose. I resisted the urge to snap to attention. "Ah, Boisjoly. No, going to the conservatory. Why? What's in the gallery?"

"You promised to show it to me," I said. "It's been years since I was last there. I'd be most gratified to reacquaint myself with some of the marvels that I remember, and be introduced to any that you've added."

The major appraised me with an arched eyebrow of the sort that precedes observations like 'we may make a soldier of you yet, young man.'

"Ah, yes, indeed," he said. "Certainly, Mister Boisjoly. Only too glad."

We walked in silence to the foyer and then up to the first floor to the great oak door of the gallery. The major swung it open and an Aladdin's cave of wonders hove into view before us.

"You still don't keep it locked, Major?" I asked.

"Nothing here of any value to anyone who hasn't served his country," he said, with a hoarse nostalgia.

The gallery did indeed have a decidedly martial theme to it. There were swords on display racks, some ceremonial, with engravings on their lustrous blades, some that had served more practical use, and were now rusted, bent and, at one point and another, bloody. There were sidearms under glass, including duelling pistols and an old Webley Revolver that still gleamed dully under a film of machine oil. Four rifles — an elephant gun, a short gun, a Musketoon personal defence rifle, and a flintlock, complete with fixed bayonet — leaned in formation in a corner. There were native shields and spears fixed to the wall, bows and arrows, spurs, riding crops, and countless daggers, stilettos, kirpans and katars. Troop photographs and illustrations depicting the entirety of the eastern empire cluttered the walls, and countless medals were pinned onto a worn Union Jack in a vitrine.

Only one side of one wall, next to the door, had anything like a domestic flavour, with posed photographs of the households that had welcomed the major. This included a photograph of Canterfell Hall in its glory days, with a cast of family and domestic staff that made the picture look like a promotional still from one of DW Griffith's epic adventures. Beneath that were similarly staged photographs before pagodas and bungalows, dated during the heyday of the Raj and signed by his hosts, mostly local luminaries like Lord Major Scott Waring-Bigelow and Lady Bigelow, Baig Samir and Begum Maya Badhani, and the Right Reverend Digby "Digs" Copdock, Bishop of Rangoon.

"I believe that this is what you came to see," said the major. He'd led the way into the room and now stood behind a small plinth, on top of which was a brass and rosewood box with a pyramid lid. It looked like a complex sort of construction, and appeared to have considerably more brass fixtures than its size and presumed purpose might warrant. It looked like an arrogant sort of box, as though it knew a secret and wasn't telling.

"Most impressive, Major," I said. "Does it do anything?"

"It's a box, Boisjoly," said the major. "What do you think it does?"

"Holds things?"

"That is its chief and only function, yes." The major bent over the box and manipulated with both hands hidden levers on either side. A clean, satisfying 'click' emanated from somewhere deep within the apparatus. Next, the major depressed what had appeared to be a mere decorative feature on the top of the pyramid, and the lid popped up with another satisfying sound, this time more like a 'boing'. The major opened the lid the rest of the way and presented the purple silk interior, like a magician performing the reveal of his signature illusion.

Inside the box was, on immediate inspection, some debris.

"Ah," I said. "Very, uh, quite. Indeed."

"This one," said the major, pointing at what looked like a stone of some particularly valueless mineral, "is from the Khyber Pass."

"Is it now?" I said.

"You were expressing an interest, were you not?" said the

major, and I knew in that same instant what I was looking at.

"And this would be the arrowhead from Mandalay," I said, nodding sagely at a triangle of slate.

The major shook his head with a gratified smile. My inability to distinguish ordinance that had been inside his body was bringing him the satisfaction of the ardent collector.

"No sir," he said. "Agrah. Left shoulder. This one is Mandalay." The major indicated a chip of stone that might have been flint but could, in my opinion, very well have been the tip of an arrowhead. "Ah, no," he said. "Quite right, other way round."

"Most extraordinary," I said. "Tell me, Major, was the inspector able to search the gallery to his satisfaction? I would have thought that it would present untold challenges to the uninitiated."

"The room holds no secrets for the constable," said the major. "He's been here many times."

The major carefully closed the lid of the ornate chest, and it sealed itself with a series of delicate clicks and whirs, as gears and bolts spun back into place somewhere deep within the mechanism. And then a most peculiar thing happened.

The major and I both distinctly heard a disembodied voice say; "Keep this locked from now on, will you?" as though from within the box. We looked at each other and then back down at the box, which then said, "Yes, Inspector."

The major and I glanced at the speaking tube. Ivor and Hug were one floor above us, in the study.

"You're quite sure that you heard nothing yesterday morning, Major, during the unfortunate incident," I asked.

The major fixed me with that quizzical expression of which I had seen so much since arriving at Canterfell Hall, giving the impression that he had forgotten who I was.

"Certainly possible. Not a young man anymore, you know."

I moved to the window and looked down at the garden. The first floor of the tower, presumably for sound considerations relevant to household security in the eleventh century, was a good twenty feet from the ground, and the second floor another twenty feet above that. This afforded an excellent view of the point at which Sebastian Canterfell's spirit was returned to the manufacturer, and of the grounds and forest beyond. A shallow valley formed by the river created an artistic depression in the thicket, exposing the thatched roof of the Hare's Foot Inn and Tavern set against the rolling fields of fertile Sussex farmland.

As the crow flies, the village of Fray is a stone's throw from the borders of the estate. If one is neither a crow nor a stone, however, the journey is a circuitous but pleasantly bucolic walk along country roads to the ancient stone bridge from which one all but doubles back the same distance, circumnavigating the woods. At any time of the year, day or night and in all weather, the route is a moving picture of pastoral England, leafy and lush and majestic. On a summer's day in July, however, with blossoms hurling their perfume at you from all directions, birds singing hallelujah in the trees, gentle breezes shifting the leaves in light applause, the soil and its issue bursting with clamour and colour, and the sun bathing it all in warmth and devotion, the combined effect is the last thing mortal eyes need behold.

After the bridge, the road is forest on one side and rolling, waving, fields of grain on the other. It was early afternoon, which apparently was when those who do such things drive horses built like breweries across their fields, reaping winter wheat. It was also the right time of day for the forest to echo with small arms fire, as hunters from as far as London and Hastings descended on Fray to participate in the rich tradition of murdering woodland creatures en masse.

The Hare's Foot Inn stands at the frontier of the village like a customs house, delineating what amounts to civilisation from the wilds of Canterfell Wood. The split rock foundation probably predates the tower of Canterfell Hall, and there are species of grass and insect unknown anywhere in the world outside of the thatched roof of the long, low main building. The original structure was designed to meet the challenges of the age in which it was built, and its walls are two feet of accumulated history and its timbered ceilings sag in the centre such that one has to bend almost double to see from one end of the tavern to the other.

"Mister Boisjoly," called List Porter, the landlord, with equal parts pomp and circumstance.

"Hello Porter," I said, sidling up to the fond, old counter, formed of oak from Fray Wood and iron from Fray blacksmith. The interior of the tavern was of the cool, quiet, eternal twilight found in all the best pubs regardless of the hour or season. The only source of light was slices of sunshine that sneaked through the cracks to find and illuminate lazy particles of dust. The pub was empty but for Porter and myself, as it would be, with the entirety of its clientele working their fields.

List was much like his pub — he was squat and friendly and welcoming, and he had been a fixture in Fray for as long as I had known the place. He had little thatching on the roof, but he had always compensated for that with a cloth cap and the sort of wily obsequiousness that men with cloth caps tend to have in buckets.

"Thank you, Porter," I said, in recognition of the clay tankard of ruby bitter that landed on the bar, in a close tie with my elbow doing the same. The bartop was much beloved but would have been replaced a hundred years ago were it in one of those cosmopolitan public houses, where old-fashioned notions of custom and tradition have long ago ceded ground to the myopic ends of commerce and hygiene. Consequently, the surface leaned, somewhat, toward the customer, and Porter would habitually under-pour every pint to the precise measure necessary to prevent spillage. The difference between that which we drank and that for which we paid was universally agreed to be a sort of heritage tax.

"I'd heard you were back at the castle," said Porter. I had assumed as much, because Porter occupied the organic centre of a rhizomatic information network, the dichotomy of which was that he somehow knew more and knew it sooner than any of his sources. "Nasty business with Mister Sebastian. What do you make of this Inspector Wittersham? Closed mouth sort of chap, if you ask me, but you get that with these London coppers, particularly your academics. They spend less time as a bobby, you see, never develop the knack for easy terms with the community. Just three years in uniform he did, mostly in Putney but for a summer in Richmond."

"Every bit as refreshing as I remember it, Porter," I said. I had been reacquainting myself with Hare's Foot Best Bitter while he spoke.

"Get it while you can, Mister Boisjoly," said Porter, idly caressing the tap. "I expect this is the last brewing season."

"Are you mad, Porter?" I asked. "Of course it isn't. There'll be a Hare's Foot Best Bitter long after you've been hanged. Why would you say such a thing?"

"The river, Mister Boisjoly," he said, with a dark finality. "Without the honest waters of Fray Brook, the brew won't be the same. Might be better, I suppose, with municipal water, but it won't be Hare's Foot Best Bitter. I'll have to change the name, of course. What do you think of 'Porter's Best Effort'?"

"I believe I can put your mind to rest, Porter," I said. "I saw Fray Brook not an hour ago, and it was in the best of health. Flowing with the vigour of a river half its age."

"For now, perhaps," said Porter. "But as soon as they break ground on the new development, the river is bound to be dredged. Or buried. At the very least diverted. It's what they do, these London property developers, they have a ferocious prejudice against nature." He said 'London property developers' as a single taxonomy, like 'English House Sparrow'. "You show one of these London property developers a tree, they go into a blind rage, they do, and before you know it, they'll have it down and replaced with a terraced townhouse."

"You still think that's going through, then, in spite of what's happened?"

Porter took my tankard and reflexively pumped it full again, while simultaneously managing to shake his head despairingly.

"It's already started, Mister Boisjoly," he said. "Them fellows are down here almost every week, now. Let me tell you what sort of men we're talking about — they go into the woods, they measure things, shift my traps, shoot pigeons off my roof, hammer stakes in the ground and tie them together with bits of string. They're mad as caged bats, Mister Boisjoly. And they have no regard for nature."

"I expect they're surveying... hold up, they shoot pigeons off your roof?"

"They come down for the hunting, but they make no distinction between pigeons on my roof and pheasants in the forest," said Porter. "They deny it, of course, just as they deny their plan to poison the river, but you can't trust no one from London, anyone will tell you that."

Porter knocked earnestly on the bar, concluding the case for the prosecution like a seasoned barrister, and looked at me for judgement. An awkward silence ensued.

"Present company excepted, of course," he hastily appended to his summation.

"No offence taken, I assure you," I said. "We're a frightful pack of barbarians."

"Mister Boisjoly," said Porter, leaning earnestly across the bar, "they drink their beer in half pints."

"Do you even sell half pints?"

"Have to serve it in jam jars."

"Still, that was all before the unfortunate demise of Mister Sebastian," I said. "I expect Hal or Fiddles will be managing things in future, and they may not be so keen on developing Canterfell Wood."

"I hadn't considered that, Mister Boisjoly," said Porter, with a wooden affectation strongly suggestive of someone who has, indeed, considered that. "I hate to find any good in the misfortunes of others, but I suppose you may very well be right." He put both elbows on the bar and fixed me with the look of a man prepared for a frank exchange of ideas. "What's it all about then, eh? I heard Mister Sebastian was chucked off the tower by someone looking for the codicil."

"Who said that?"

"Spooner, the postman," said Porter. "Heard it at the post

office, who got it from that shifty Mister Lydde bloke from the castle."

"What about this codicil, Porter? Yesterday was the first I'd heard of it."

"Story is, the major wrote it years ago, while he was out east — India or the Malaya or some such place, defending British interests. He sent it back home with a trusted fellow officer, a captain, at the time. The captain presents his compliments at the castle, and stays on a bit and, while on the premises, hides the document somewhere about the place."

"But, why?"

"He wanted to alter his last will and testament, Mister Boisjoly."

"Thank you, Porter," I said. "That neatly dispenses with the self-evident, but I mean why go to all the trouble of confidential couriers and secret hiding places?"

"I can't really say for certain, but I assume it's for the obvious reason — in case he were to die in India. He wanted to change his will in a way that nobody knew about until after he was gone."

"That appears to be the central theme, Porter. That which Aristotle, were he here with us now, would call the 'big idea' — what does the codicil say?"

"I'll give you my opinion, if you want it."

"I do, and I would cherish it always."

"It don't say nothing at all."

"How's that? Do you mean to suggest that the major sent a trusted confidant on a journey of twenty thousand miles to hide a blank piece of paper in the walls of Canterfell Hall?"

"In a word, Mister Boisjoly, yes."

"I suppose it makes as much sense as any other theory I've

heard so far," I conceded. "But why would he do such a thing?"

"Why, to keep the family on its toes, of course," said Porter. "Say you have a fortune coming to you, if you abide by certain conditions, but you don't know what the conditions are."

"I see what you mean," I agreed. "I'd tread a narrow path."

"Exactly."

"Tell me, Porter, did you know that there was an earldom associated with Fray?"

"Of course."

"Yes, of course you did. Did you know that it was in abeyance?"

"I did."

"And that it was being restored?"

"I didn't know that it was final, sir. I regard this as very good news for the village. Honestly, sir, it was a source of some considerable embarrassment to myself and others what live in this town that our earldom was withdrawn under such a cloud."

"Withdrawn? I was given to understand that it was in abeyance until clear title could be established by a male heir."

"That is very nearly the case, sir."

"But not entirely."

"Put another way, sir, not at all," said Porter. "The title is in abeyance until the earldom is officially pardoned by the king."

"Pardoned? For what offence?"

"Treason," said Porter, as though the word was a salty and delicious snack. "Another pint?"

"I will, Porter, and have one for yourself."

Porter pulled two more perfect underpours.

"Pray continue, Porter," I said, taking up my tankard. "Picking up roughly around the part where you said the word 'treason'."

"It was around 1485, I believe, and the Wars of the Roses was just winding down."

"I recall," I said. "Glorious time to be alive."

"Henry Tudor was on his way home from France, with a view to giving a right spanking to Richard of York."

"And he passed through Fray? I thought he landed in Wales."

"That he did sir," confirmed Porter with a nod, "but loyalists to the Tudor claim petitioned the earl, along with many others, to join Henry on the field of battle."

"But he didn't?"

"According to legend, no, he did not."

"Could one just refuse to join up?" I asked. "Wasn't that the same as picking sides?"

"He didn't refuse. He avoided the issue by way of a clever ruse." Porter posed his tankard as an illustrative prop, playing the role of Canterfell Hall. "The village of Fray was, at the time and much as it is now, composed of farmland surrounding the castle. There was a small standing army, a few knights and a local militia that owed its loyalty to the earl, but the population was mainly farmers, one very much like the next."

"What was the nature of this ruse, Porter?" I asked, though I felt that I had already gleaned something approaching a full picture.

"The earl took to the fields, dressed as a commoner, and let it be understood that he and his army had already ridden on to join Henry's rebellion."

"Are you saying that when called upon to do his duty for

England, the Third Earl of Fray pretended that he wasn't home?"

"Neatly put, Mister Boisjoly," said Porter, taking up his pint. "Yes."

"Obviously I applaud the development, if only because it puts a smile on your rugged face," I said, "but why would the title be restored now?"

"Somebody with a claim needs to petition for it," said Porter. "If no one asked, it wouldn't be done."

"I understand that Fiddles petitioned on behalf of the major."

"There you go, then."

"But why would it be approved?" I asked. "Surely some Canterfell has begged forgiveness prior to now."

"Politics would be my guess," said Porter. "It's always politics, from before the Wars of the Roses."

"Are you referring to the seat in the House of Lords?"

"I am, sir," said Porter. "I expect that for Mister Baldwin, the prime minister, the earldom of Fray is another Conservative vote in the Lords."

"Assuming the major takes his seat."

"Well, the major's not a young man, if it's not being indelicate. They probably thought they'd be making an earl of Mister Sebastian."

"But now it'll go to Halliwell Canterfell, who's already a member of parliament."

"Exactly so, sir, but doubtless you know that nobility are barred from holding a seat in parliament," said Porter. "Which means, ironically, that instead of gaining a vote in the Lords, Mister Baldwin is losing a vote in Parliament."

"But not gaining one in the Lords?"

"Mister Halliwell?" said Porter. "Not on your life, sir. He

wouldn't sit in the Lords if he was marched there at gunpoint."

"Even were he to lose his seat in Parliament?"

"Even then," said Porter, nodding. "Which, of course, was bound to happen anyway, once that new development takes hold, and what was once a Conservative safe seat is beset with Labour voters from London."

"Is that what Halliwell said, Porter?" I asked, and looked pointedly about the empty tavern.

"No, well, yes, not in so many words, you understand."

"Why don't we ask him, then," I said. I put down my empty tankard, waited one dramatic beat, and then another, and then I looked the landlord in the eye. "Come along, Porter, I know that Halliwell Canterfell, the honourable member for Fray, is staying here at the inn."

CHAPTER TEN
The Continuing Consequences of the Norman Conquest

Halliwell Canterfell, the honourable member for Fray, was wearing pyjamas.

He was sitting barefoot on the grassy grade that descended from the back of the Hare's Foot to the treeline, and he was looking vaguely in the direction of the castle. He was every inch the Canterfell, from the aristocratically weak chin to the noble bald spot, but he had the carriage of a man who forgets to eat and that, combined with an infrequently exercised and randomly applied shaving routine, gave the parliamentarian something of the air of a hobo.

There was a pewter tray next to him on the grass with a full English tea, and he was forcefully blowing the steam off a cup that appeared to have long gone cold. It was a fanciful scene, and neither a March Hare nor a Mad Hatter would have been remotely out of place.

"Good afternoon, Mister Canterfell," I said.

"Hello, young man." Halliwell looked at me with a vacant smile and laughing eyes, and he wiggled his toes in the grass.

"I wonder if you remember me, sir," I said. "Anthony

Boisjoly. I was at school with your son."

Halliwell nodded solemnly. "I knew your father."

"I'm afraid he's passed away," I said.

"Who got him?" asked the honourable member, a confidential squint to his eye. "The fascists? Or the Knights Templar?"

Which was well within the range of the expected, for those who know Halliwell Canterfell. It's broadly understood that the nation's asylums are only able to operate as efficiently as they do because parliament is there to take the most acute cases off their hands. And it's commonly known that a reliable measure of the depth of a man's psychosis is the duration of his career in the House of Commons. Halliwell Canterfell had been returned to Westminster by the good people of Fray a record five times. On each occasion it was a landslide.

"Neither," I answered. "Papa fell under an electric tram by Wormwood Scrubs."

"Poor chap," sympathised Halliwell. "They always get you."

"Well, at least he died doing what he loved most," I said, with Christian forbearance, "stumbling drunkenly through Shepherd's Bush." I took the liberty of a patch of grass next to the tea tray. "Talking of foreshortened journeys, I take it you know that there's been an unfortunate turn of events at Canterfell Hall."

The honourable member nodded. "Sebastian's been thrown out a window," he said. "What an extraordinary thing. There must be a dozen easier ways to kill a man. I think, had it been me, I'd have poisoned him. Or run him through with one of Father's swords. Or simply hit him over the head with something. A paving stone, for instance. Yes, a paving stone would serve very nicely."

"It's human nature to over-complicate simple things," I said. "Might I ask why you're here, Mister Canterfell?"

"Constituency business," he said. "Meet the voters, count the badgers — makes a break from the affairs of the nation."

"Of course," I sympathised. "But I meant, why are you staying at the inn, rather than at Canterfell Hall?"

"Don't much care for Canterfell Hall, in point of fact," he said. "Far too many Canterfells for my liking. How did you know I was here?"

"You were bending the ear last night of one Inspector Wittersham. He was very interested in your views regarding Edmund Ironside."

"To the one true king," said Halliwell, raising his teacup in a toast.

"Hear, hear," I said, narrowly avoiding a charge of sedition by not actually raising a cup. "I think the inspector's going to want to have a few words with you about what happened to your brother."

"I'm not sure that would be wise," said the honourable member, adding in a lower tone, "We didn't really get along, Sebastian and I."

"I expect that'll be the sort of thing the inspector would want to discuss," I suggested. "However, an examination of the scene of the crime indicates that the assassin wanted something."

"Yes. He wanted to throw Sebastian out a window."

"I mean, something else."

"You don't think that's enough?"

"Quite possibly, but some people are never satisfied," I said. "There's been some suggestion that the object of a thorough search of Sebastian's study was the Canterfell codicil."

"Ah." Halliwell turned toward me and sat cross-legged on the grass. "Have they found it?"

"I'm afraid not," I said. "And it would appear that the major can shed no light on the contents."

"Of course not," said Halliwell. "He didn't write it."

"This is new," I said. "So far I've been told there's no codicil, that there is a codicil, but it's blank, that it requires your son and Hal to serve in the military, and that its purpose is to explicitly exclude your sister-in-law from inheriting, but all competing theories have so far involved the major. Even the theory that says that the codicil is fictional is founded on the view that your father made it up."

The honourable member fixed me with a cagey squint, just short of a wink. "The codicil was written by Elmer Bunce, Third Earl of Fray."

"You've seen it?"

"No," he shook his head sadly. "I have not. Its contents, however, have been a matter of family lore for generations."

"The major says he has no recollection of it," I pointed out.

"If that's so, then I'm the only person alive who has," said Halliwell. He looked to the skies with an expression of awe. "Sebastian had it last. He was meant to pass it along to that weedy one, the lad with no chin."

"Harold. Your nephew."

"That's it. Harold. Eldest son is meant to reveal the codicil to eldest son."

"It would appear that Sebastian didn't get the chance. Do you know what it says, at least?"

"Of course," said Halliwell. "It unifies the earldom of Fray."

"Is the earldom in need of unifying?"

"Oh, very much so." The honourable member clasped his hands together in a gesture that seemed intended to hold back the torrent. He took a breath and then spoke in measured tones. "The earldom was withdrawn, you see, because of Elmer Bunce's failure to support the claim of Henry Tudor, pretender to the throne."

"I understand that he settled on a strategy of cautious neutrality."

"Neutrality? Not at all. The earl very firmly fixed his banner to the cause of Edouard Adeling."

"Not Richard of York."

"Of course not," the honourable member scoffed, as he would had I proposed that the earl had taken up the cause of the sea in its famous dispute with King Cnut. "Edouard Adeling, direct heir to Edmund Ironside, and sovereign of the realm."

"Is it too late to get a programme?" I asked. "I've never heard of Edouard Adeling."

"And you never will," said Halliwell. "Adeling died without issue, doubtless of a broken heart. But not without first rewarding the loyalty of those who stood by him."

"Which brings us, I take it, to the codicil."

"It does," said Halliwell. "When the title is restored, the codicil can be invoked, and all the lands and chattels promised to Elmer Bunce, Third Earl of Fray, will be joined to the earldom."

"What are these lands and chattels?"

"Well, there's the castle and the village. The surrounding fields, of course," said the honourable member, "and Normandy."

"The Normandy in France?"

"It's the only one I know of, but if there are others I

suppose they might be included too. I don't know all the details."

"Just to put a clear line under it, Mister Canterfell," I said. "You're saying that much of northern France belongs to the earldom of Fray."

"Rightfully and, in my view as a legislator, legally."

"I see," I lied. "You must be very anxious to secure the codicil."

"Why would I be?"

"If it's not being indelicate, sir," I said. "With the passing of your brother, you're next in line for the title, after the major. But perhaps you didn't know — the earldom is to be restored."

"Makes no difference to me," said the honourable member. "I'm the honourable member for Fray. That's title enough for me."

"You don't wish to become the Fifth Earl of Fray... and Normandy?"

"Let Fairfax do all that. I'd have to give up my seat in parliament."

"Awfully unfair, isn't it, that hereditary peers can't serve in parliament," I said, sympathetically.

"Positively archaic."

As mentioned, the curtain of countryside offered by Fray and its fields is of that rich, textured, English landscape that is key to the wealth of the language. It's generally understood that the reason the French lack a word for 'lush' is that they don't need one, and while it is so that the German vocabulary once contained an expression amounting to 'Edenic' it was long ago discarded, out of frustration. The word 'pastorale' holds an equivalent meaning for Italians, but it is known that they only ever use it when visiting Surrey. Conversely, authorities of the classics are in general agreement that, were it not for the incomparable beauty of rural England, Shakespeare, when chronicling the adventures of Richard II, would have dispensed with 'sceptred isles' and 'precious stones' in 'silver seas', 'this blessed plot', 'this earth' and 'this realm', and simply written 'England' and left it at that.

Add to that a pleasantly sunny summer afternoon and you've already got a delightful meander along a country path from the village to Canterfell Hall, but once you've applied three thick layers of Hare's Foot Best Bitter, you've really begun to see what Shakespeare was getting at. Consequently, I didn't rush, and nevertheless caught up to a man with a goat.

I surmised instantly that this was the gardener of Canterfell Hall. The identity of the goat could be investigated at a later date, but I suspected that it was the errant animal who had been so conspicuously negligent of his duties to the grounds of the castle.

"Hallo," I called, slowing my gait. The gardener — a thin, fragile type who looked like he'd fallen from the stick on which he'd been posted to warn off the crows — was directing his entire weight toward the castle, and it was being countered by a rope attached to a small white goat whose interests appeared to lie elsewhere. It was a hot day and the gardener was overdressed for it in coveralls and a flannel shirt, high Wellingtons, and a cloud of bees which he shared with the goat. The poor man gleamed with sweat, and every time he gained ground against the goat he would lose it as he liberated a hand to wave away the insects.

"Anthony Boisjoly," I said. "I'm staying at the castle. Can I be of assistance?"

"You can kill this goat for me," said the gardener through clenched teeth.

"It would be an immense pleasure," I said. "But I feel that it's a rash act that we'd both regret, in time. Allow me to make a counter-proposal, if you'll bear with me a moment."

I left the gardener to stare in wonder after me as I leapt the culvert to the wheat field which traces the edge of the road, where I pulled up several long stalks of ripe grain. The goat had deduced my plan before the gardener had, and it was approaching me with a most amiable attitude before I'd even leapt back to the road. In a matter of moments the three of us were making excellent time, and both goat and gardener were in much improved, if not jovial spirits.

"I'm Mallet, sir," said my travelling companion. "Gardener at Canterfell Hall."

"So I gathered," I said. "You must be pleased to have found your goat."

"If I might be permitted to speak freely, sir, no, I'm not," said Mallet earnestly. He was clearly moved by some earlier actions of the animal. "It's Mister Canterfell, God bless his immortal soul, what wants the goat to do the gardening. It's Mister Canterfell, God bless his immortal soul, sir, what ought to have explained that to the goat, in this man's opinion."

"I would have thought it would have been in his nature. The goat's, that is."

"T'is," said Mallet. "The beast will eat most anything, but it lacks what you might call discretion. I just now found it at the church, grazing on the grave yard."

"Saint George's Church?" I marvelled. "Isn't that near the station? How ever did you find it?"

"I tracked it by the animal's unique aroma, sir," said

Mallet. "It's surprisingly easy to follow, once you know what it is."

"Ah," I said, meaning it. "That's the goat, is it? I thought that the field had been freshly fertilised."

"Too late in the season for that, sir," said Mallet. "And manure, comparatively speaking, is quite pleasant."

"How do the bees tolerate it, then?"

"Them aren't bees, sir, them are hoverflies — black and yellow hoverflies, as unlike bees as you can get, apart from that. They don't tolerate the smell of goat, they like it." Mallet shook his head in sympathy for this miasma of cursed souls.

"Very well, then, how do you tolerate it?"

"Not wishing to find good in the misfortunes of others," he answered, with the tone of one about to find good in the misfortune of others, "but I had hoped that with the passing of Mister Sebastian, God bless his immortal soul, some similar end might come to the goat."

"I've been meaning to ask you about that, Mallet," I said. "Have you spoken to the police yet with regards to the events of yesterday?"

"I have sir, yes."

"Excellent. What did they ask you?"

"They asked me not to speak to you, sir."

"Really? By name?"

"Do not speak to that Boisjoly chap," said Mallet. "That inspector fellow from London said it."

"Not Hug, though."

"No, not the constable."

"I suppose it's a little late, now," I said. "The goat has already intervened to bring us together, and here we are talking."

"I guess that's true," said Mallet. "They asked me what I saw, and I told them."

"And what did you see?"

"I was in the garden, by the lake. I saw Mister Sebastian come flying out the second-floor window of the tower."

"Did you see anything else? Hear anything?"

"Just Mister Sebastian begging for his life. I looked just as he come shooting out the window, like slop out of a sluice gate."

"That's an exceptional vantage point, the lake. You can see the conservatory from there, unless I'm mistaken."

"You're not, sir, if the conservatory is that greenhouse with no plants in it."

"That's the place," I confirmed. "Did you see who was there?"

"I did," said Mallet, nodding. "Mister Vickers."

"Excellent, Mallet. Did you tell the inspector this?" I asked. "It corresponds with Mister Fairfax's accounting, with which the inspector has taken issue."

"I did sir, yes."

"And what did the inspector say?" I asked.

"That likely I'd be called to testify at Mister Canterfell's murder trial."

"Troubling," I said. "Did he say why?"

"No, and I didn't wish to give no offence by asking," said Mallet. "But he made note of what he called the timing of events."

"Timing, you say."

"Yes sir. Most particularly when Mister Fairfax left the conservatory, and when Mister Sebastian begin pleading for his life, a good five minutes later."

"Roughly the time it would take someone to get from the conservatory to the study."

"I expect that's what the inspector was reckoning, yes."

"It's been an uplifting stroll, Mister Mallet, and I thank you for it," I said, as we reached the gravel drive leading to the house. "And I hope for my part that I've contributed in some small way to the healing of divisions between you and your goat. Here is where I leave you, though, to see if I can't save you the trouble and embarrassment of testifying against Fairfax Canterfell at his trial for murder."

"Just the lad I hoped to see, Hal," I said. On a hunch, I had gone to the terrace, from whence he had witnessed his father's demise. He was in a wicker armchair, making notes in the margin of a book that, to my mind, was quite full enough already.

"Hullo, Anty," said Hal, only barely looking up.

"Hal," I said. "I require your undivided attention."

He put his pencil in the book, closed it, and leaned over it at me.

"I have a very important question about the murder of your father," I said.

"What is it?"

"Do you recall the inscription on the back of the painting of Melpomene?"

"The inscription? On the back of the painting?"

"Of Melpomene," I confirmed. "Yes."

"Of course," he said. "But why?"

"If I'm entirely honest, Hal, it's a rather circuitous line of reasoning, which I expect to shortly be explaining to the inspector. You're welcome to sit in then."

"Very well," sighed Hal. "It's a rather amateurish bit of love poetry..." He sat back and looked up and to the left, as though hoping to find it written there. Then recited,

"My muse, my love, my heart's begun

"My Melpomene, my goddess, my forbidden one"

There was a strange beauty to the silence which followed.

"Are you quite certain, Hal?"

"I am, yes," he said. "It's badly faded with the years, and the hand-writing was hardly in the monastic tradition, but that's what it says."

"It's worse than I'd imagined," I said. "And I was imagining something in which butterflies and buttercups featured prominently."

"I know," agreed Hal. "We don't speak of it."

"Sound policy," I said. "You're quite sure that's how it goes, '...my heart's begun'?"

"Quite sure," said Hal. "That phrase in particular has a certain tenacity."

I brooded on this at some length. I was unsurprised by the inventory of inspirations — the muses and Melpomenes and what-have-you — but I found the lyric disappointingly short on concrete information.

Then I realised that I had the wrong end of the bat, and the identity hidden behind the painting was not that of Melpomene, but of the mysterious 'my'. And then I said "Ah, Vickers," because Vickers had just entered, stage left.

"Good afternoon, sir," said Vickers, with what I'm sure was a twinkle of recognition. It was quite moving.

"Vickers, we're going to organise a tray of drinks in the conservatory," I said. "And when we've done that, would you be so good as to invite the inspector, Mister Fairfax, and Mrs Canterfell to join me there."

"Very good, sir," said Vickers. "I rather expect that the inspector will insist on some justification."

"Yes, of course, Vickers. Tell him that I've solved the murder of Sebastian Canterfell."

CHAPTER ELEVEN
The Suspicious Circumstance of the Sealed Study

Hug had his notepad at the ready.

Ivor was lighting his pipe with an elaborate pantomime that elevated the mundane act to an expression of profound impatience. Fairfax was mixing drinks with the same noisy *joie de vivre* that I myself might show if I believed I were about to be absolved of a capital offence. Laetitia was standing in a shadow of her own making, in spite of the sun shimmering through the glass roof of the conservatory. Hal was idling by the window, still absorbed in his book.

I took my whisky and soda and a position by the sideboard, where the painting of Melpomene had once hung.

"The key, Inspector," I said, "is who heard what, and when they heard it."

Ivor looked at me through the rising fumes of his pipe and blew smoke out the corner of his mouth.

"Hug?" I said. "What do your notes say that Mister Vickers heard, just before Sebastian Canterfell stepped into the void?"

"Mister Vickers said that he heard the deceased shouting

at someone to leave the study."

"To leave, you say," I said.

"Yes, Mister Boisjoly."

"And Fiddles," I said. "What do you believe that you heard from outside the door?"

"Uncle Sebastian was telling me to fetch the keys."

"Just as I thought," I said. "And I understand that Mister Mallet, the gardener, heard something else altogether."

"Mister Mallet reports hearing the deceased pleading for his life," said Hug.

"Mister Mallet," I repeated, "heard Sebastian Canterfell pleading for his life, just before being launched into the garden."

"Yes, sir," confirmed Hug.

"Meanwhile, the major, Mrs Canterfell, and the below-stairs staff, claim to have heard nothing at all."

Hug referred once again to his notes, turned a page, then another, and then said, "Correct."

"I dispute all these accounts," I said. "The below-stairs staff heard nothing because the speaking tube had been blocked with a potato."

"And the major?" said Ivor. "And Mrs Canterfell? They also say they heard nothing."

"Forgive me Inspector, but no, they didn't," I said. "What they said was that they heard only the fall. They said that because they did not witness the crime, and were in fact guessing."

"Are you calling me a liar, Mister Boisjoly?" said Laetitia, her arms crossed for battle.

"My dear Mrs Canterfell, of course not. I'm merely calling you a bad guesser."

"Based on what, Mister Boisjoly?" asked Ivor.

"The testimony of Vickers, Fiddles, and Mallet, who all heard something they thought sounded, respectively, like 'leave', 'keys', and 'please'."

"But you dispute that, too, I take it," said Ivor.

"The word they heard, Inspector, was 'bees'."

"Bees."

"Bees, Inspector. The entire Canterfell clan is fiercely allergic to bees. One sting and they become violently ill. Two stings and they require immediate medical attention. Three or more stings would certainly kill the most stout of Canterfell men. Isn't that so, Fiddles?"

"Oh, rather," said Fiddles. "Do you remember, Hal, when we were forced to jump off Hythe Bridge?"

"Yes," confirmed Hal, and then explained to the congregation, "A bumblebee had taken a keen interest in my ice lolly."

"Mister Boisjoly," said Ivor, "while it's true that the coroner has yet to make an official finding, I can say with some certainty that Mister Canterfell was not killed by bee stings."

"Yes he was, in a manner of speaking," I said. "He leapt from the second floor of the tower to escape a swarm of bees. He took a running jump at his best chance — the reflecting pool. He knew that he was more likely to survive the fall than a hundred bee stings."

"Why didn't he just leave by the door?" asked Ivor. "Are you suggesting that he was in too great a panic to simply turn the key?"

"The chief characteristic of a locked-room mystery, that which is at the root of its broad appeal, is that the room is locked from the inside," I explained. "Everyone, including the presumed killer, is locked out, rendering the murder seemingly impossible."

"As was the case of the study," observed Ivor.

"Yes, but not only was everyone else locked out, but the victim was locked in. Sebastian Canterfell didn't unlock the door, Inspector, because he couldn't," I said. "Did it not strike you as odd that in spite of the not inconsiderable abuse the door took at the hands of two strong men and an iron hand cannon weighing in excess of two hundred pounds, the key remained in the door?"

"Of course," said Hug. "It must have got stuck."

"It was stuck, Hug," I said. "But I doubt that our killer was counting on such a turn of good fortune. I believe that if you examine the lock you'll see that it's been tampered with, and I'm prepared to offer odds that you'll find it's been filled with carpet glue."

"I say, the carpet," said Ivor. "It was pulled up. Is it your contention that Sebastian Canterfell was searching his own study when he was interrupted by a swarm of bees?"

"No, Inspector," I said. "It is my view that the study wasn't searched at all. I think it far more likely that what appears to us to be evidence of an intense search, is in fact evidence of an intense effort to avoid being stung by bees. Paintings were torn from the walls to be used to swat the insects, and the carpet was pulled up in an effort to use it as a shield."

"Which presumably didn't work," said Ivor.

"Manifestly not," I concurred.

"Very thorough," said Ivor. "And have you considered why there was not a single bee sting on the victim's body?"

"I have, Inspector. It's because there were no bees," I said. "Sebastian Canterfell was driven to his death by a swarm of hoverflies — standard, though strangely broad-minded, farm flies, that have evolved the uncanny defence mechanism of looking and sounding exactly like bees."

"How did a swarm of counterfeit bees get into the study?" asked Fiddles. "Could this all be just some tragic accident?"

"They were introduced into the study via the speaking tube," I said.

"How?" said Ivor. "How does one even acquire a swarm of hoverflies, never mind put them in a tube?"

"I'm unsure of the mechanics of the operation," I confessed. "But I suspect that the answer to both questions is the same — a bag of goat dung."

"I beg your pardon."

"I don't see the attraction either," I said. "But we share the dubious disadvantage of not being hoverflies. To them I expect the stuff is like a whiff of Shalimar."

"So the killer trapped hoverflies in a bag of goat dung, and then forced them into the speaking tube," said Ivor, with what I briefly imagined was a trace of doubt.

"But first taking the precaution of dropping a potato into the tube, so that the insects could only go in one direction," I added. "And chasing off the goat. Again."

"Why did he chase off the goat?" asked Ivor. "And why again?" Then he reflected for a moment and added, "And what goat?"

"The gardening goat," I explained. "Hoverflies adore him. This is the chief point on which they and the gardener differ. The goat needed to be removed from the premises before the flies were released into the study, or they would have immediately sought him out, undermining the effect."

"How would they have known that the goat was on the premises?"

"I can assure you, Inspector, they'd know," I said. "The gardener was able to track the animal all the way to the church."

"That's near the station," observed Hug.

"I'm led to understand that goats do not do things in half-measures," I replied.

"Constable, did you see these hoverflies in the study when you opened the door?" asked Ivor.

"No, sir," said Hug.

"It was an hour and a half later," I said. "Doubtless they were pining for their goat. The window was open and there was little to hold their interest in the study."

"Assuming that all of this is true," said Ivor, "this means that the culprit was in the gallery at eleven o'clock."

Hug drew in a sharp breath. "The major killed Sebastian Canterfell?"

"No, Hug, the major was not in the gallery at the time of the murder," I said.

Hug rifled through his notes.

"Begging your pardon, Mister Boisjoly," he said. "He was."

"No, Hug, and I admire your faith in human nature very much — heaven knows I've benefited from it in my time — but the major was something other than truthful regarding his whereabouts at the time of the murder."

"Where was he then?" asked Ivor. "Why did he lie?"

Laetitia was looking at her feet, now, and raised her head to speak.

"He was lost," I said. Laetitia shot me a glance that, were it a sound, would have been 'huh?'.

"Lost?" said Ivor.

"It's a big place."

"He's lived here all his life," protested the inspector.

"I see no need to be cruel, Inspector."

"Cruel?"

"Yes, rather, Inspector," added Fiddles. "The man's a

decorated officer."

"What are you talking about?" insisted Ivor.

"The major has moments, Inspector," I explained. "I'm only betraying this confidence because of the gravity of the situation. Did you know that he can't recall whether or not he even wrote a codicil?"

"Is that so?" asked Hal. "That would go a long way to explaining his evasiveness regarding its contents."

"Then where was the major?" asked the inspector. "And why did Mrs Canterfell lie? Does she have moments?"

"I expect that Mrs Canterfell was with the major," I said. "Doubtless he wandered into the old wing, forgetting that it was closed, and Mrs Canterfell, familiar with the old man's harmless eccentricities, hunted him down and then, not wishing to embarrass him, misrepresented the truth in order to support his claim that he was in the gallery."

"Yes," said Laetitia. "That's exactly what happened."

"I beg your pardon, Mrs Canterfell, but I find this all very improbable," said Ivor, rather predictably, and while he said it I turned to the sideboard and cleared the drinks tray, and hung it on the wall.

"My painting!" exclaimed Laetitia, rather in the manner in which she did when she noticed it missing, except in reverse.

"The muse," toasted Fiddles, raising his drink.

"Where did that come from?" said Ivor.

"Below-stairs," I said. "It was mixed in with the trays."

"Why?"

"The major put it there," I said. "Who can say why? It's a delicately balanced thing, the human mind. Forced to guess I'd say that, when you announced that the castle was to be searched, he took it down and hid it, to prevent you finding it."

"Why would he do that?"

"I mean no offence, Inspector," I said. "I know you well. We've shared a long and intimate train journey together, and I'd trust you with my last pound, but I expect the major thought you'd steal it."

"Steal it?" said Ivor. "That's madness."

"Now, really, Inspector," said Fiddles. "I very much hope that you can rely on your faculties in your declining years."

Ivor glared at Fiddles but said nothing, preferring instead to express himself in a singular shade of mauve.

"Very well," he said at last. "If the major didn't do it, who did kill Sebastian Canterfell?"

"That," I said, "I don't know."

"You don't know?" said Ivor, with the tone of one snatching victory from the jaws of defeat.

"You don't know?" repeated Fiddles, choking on his drink.

"Might I observe, at the risk of appearing immodest, that I've solved not one but two impenetrable mysteries in twenty-four hours," I said. "I appreciate the rousing vote of confidence, but I may require until tea-time merely to identify the motive, and it's just possible that I won't have built a case against the guilty party until well after dinner."

"I think I can help you with both of those outstanding issues, Mister Boisjoly," said Ivor. Then to Fiddles he said, "Mister Canterfell, would you care to explain why it is that you gave up your flat in London?"

"Oh, you know," said Fiddles. "One gets rather tired of the crowds, the incessant scurry and hum of the metropolis, don't you know."

"I say, steady on Fiddles," I said. The chief complaint that Fiddles had about Oxford was that it wasn't London, and as for scurry and hum, I've witnessed him fall asleep on a crowded omnibus at Christmas time.

"Isn't it so, Mister Canterfell," said Ivor, with the tone and manner of a world-weary barrister in a yellowing wig pronouncing 'If it please the court...'. "That you were forced to leave London when your uncle cut off your allowance?"

"Ah, that," said Fiddles. "I suppose that may have entered into it a bit as well, yes."

"And now that your uncle is deceased, you're free to return to London, with wealth and the prestige of a pending title, are you not, Mister Canterfell?"

"Now you mention it, yes, I suppose I am," said Fiddles, casting me a glance that looked as though it was coming from the bottom of a well. "Hadn't actually occurred to me."

"And perhaps you'd tell us, Mister Canterfell, why you did not think it worth the trouble to wire your father to inform him of his brother's passing?"

"He already knew," I said. "Mister Porter told him."

"And how does the landlord of the Hare's Foot come to know about a murder committed at Canterfell Hall?" demanded Ivor.

"He just does, Inspector," I interjected. "Some sort of trade secret, wouldn't you say, Fiddles? Like the famous fourth ingredient in Hare's Foot Best Bitter."

"Didn't you know, Anty?" said Fiddles. "It's linseed meal. He told me at Whitsun. Said it didn't matter anymore, in light of the plans to poison the river."

"I'm not interested in Hare's Foot Best Bitter," said Ivor, with an intonation like a kettle reaching a boil.

"Perhaps you should be, Inspector," I pointed out. "Mister Porter was able to keep the honourable member for Fray abreast of affairs because he's staying at the inn. Has been for a week. You shared a pint with him last night."

"Were you aware of this Constable?" Ivor said to Hug.

"Oh, yes sir," said Hug. "Mister Halliwell always stays at the Hare's Foot when he's down on constituency business."

The inspector regarded each of us with a cold austerity, as he might were he the sole adult in a roomful of idiot children.

"Very well," sighed Ivor. "Constable, please go to the inn and request that Mister Halliwell Canterfell visit the police station at his earliest possible convenience."

"Yes sir, Inspector," said Hug, and turned on his heel.

"Just a moment, Constable," said Ivor. "You may visit the inn after you've taken a statement from Fairfax Canterfell."

"I've already done so, Inspector," said Hug, folding back the pages of his notebook and putting them in evidence of this claim.

"Not under caution, Constable," said Ivor. "For the charge of the murder of Sebastian Canterfell."

"I must protest, Inspector," I said. "So far we've only established how the murder took place."

"Yes, thank you for that Mister Boisjoly," said Ivor. "It would have been difficult to prove a case for murder without knowing how it had been done. Constable, arrest this man."

"Just like old times, eh Hug?" said Fiddles, with the hollow bonhomie of a man standing in the shadow of the gallows. "You couldn't wire our barrister, could you Hal?"

"Happy to do it," said Hal. He joined Fiddles and Hug at the door and then had an afterthought, "Just, I mean, hate to bring it up... you didn't kill my father, did you, Fairfax?"

"Well, that was a departure from the script," I said, initially to myself, when Fiddles, Ivor, Hug and Hal had left.

"Did you inspect the painting?" asked Laetitia, reminding

me that she was still there and causing me to very nearly spill my drink.

"Of course not," I said. "Vickers insisted."

"Are you going to make me one of those?" she said, with a nod to my cocktail. "How did you figure it out then?"

"The trick was knowing that there was something to figure out," I said, stirring a splash of soda into a glass of whisky. "Had you left Melpomene where she was, or told the truth about where you were, I wouldn't have asked myself the meaning of the poem."

"And how do you know I wasn't in my room?" She took her drink and paced across the conservatory as though it was a stage.

"You told me," I said. "You claimed that you were in the Chartreuse Room, because if you'd said that you were in your room then Luna could have contradicted you. But Luna only needed to prepare two guest rooms — Miss Pierpoint's and my own."

"Devilish," said Laetitia, flatly. Doubtless she'd forgotten that the expression is usually 'devilishly clever'. It had been a trying day. "But if you didn't examine the painting, what informed your conclusions about the major?"

"The poem was from him to you," I said. "The clue is grammatical...

"My muse, my love, my heart's begun

"My Melpomene, my goddess, my forbidden one

"It reads more like a shopping list than a love poem: one muse, one love, one Melpomene, etc. Except for 'my heart's begun', the only past participle in a list of conspicuous nouns."

"That's the flaw you found in the prose?"

"It stood out," I said. "I can tell you as a one-time

practitioner that consistency is among the few qualities of the adolescent lyricist."

"And that led you to the major."

"It did," I said. "It made me think of a photograph that I saw in the gallery. The word is not 'begun', it's 'begum', which is 'ladyship', or something very like that, in Hindustani."

Laetitia turned back to me now, with a peculiar smile. "I don't think so."

"You don't think what, Mrs Canterfell?"

"I think it just means, 'my heart has begun'."

"Really?" I said. "How satisfyingly ironic. Then why did you hide the painting?"

"You really didn't examine it, did you?" she said.

"On my honour as a second-tier member of the Oxford rowing team," I said. "I take it there's something hidden beneath the backing paper?"

Laetitia nodded. "Another painting."

I was saved from learning any more intimate details of the life and loves of Laetitia Canterfell by, of all unlikely heroes, Lydde, who appeared at the door.

"You asked me to tell you when the post arrived, Mister Boisjoly."

"I did, Lydde, thank you very much," I said, then to Laetitia, "I regret that I must take my leave, Mrs Canterfell. I hope that I have been of some service."

The moment we were clear of the conservatory I said to Lydde, "Where is it?"

"Where's what, Mister Boisjoly?"

"The post, Lydde. I need to have a quick sort through it."

"It's been distributed, Mister Boisjoly," said Lydde, with very much the tone and timbre of a perisher, proudly confessing that he's put a brick through the window of the church.

"Distributed?" I said. "Lydde, you were meant to tell me when the post arrived, first thing."

"And that's just what I've done, isn't it? Post's not arrived until it's been distributed."

The legality of Lydde's argument had me stymied. I made a mental note to never bring suit against the man.

"Very well, Lydde," I said. "To whom did you distribute mail?"

"Just Mister Harold, sir," he said, "and Miss Pierpoint."

CHAPTER TWELVE
The Spectacular Spectacle of the Susceptible Spectacles

I had two obligations of duty to my former coxswain, as I saw it. I needed to exonerate him of the murder of his uncle, and I had to somehow prevent his ill-advised note from further souring his budding relationship with Rosalind. One doesn't like to impose oneself on the hospitality of a friend without at least stepping in when he's facing the gallows or turbulent affairs of the heart.

While there was nothing I could immediately do to absolve Fiddles of a charge of murder, I could perhaps lay the groundwork for a return to smooth relations with Rosalind when I did. I went to her room with a broad plan to argue his case, perhaps suggesting that Fiddles had a history of insanity. Or, had I seen a tear of regret in the corner of his eye when he recounted his folly? I began to think that yes, I may indeed have.

"Who is it?" called Rosalind in that somewhat vacant song that I'd already come to associate with her personality. It didn't bode well. A woman who has any regard for a man, whether she loves or detests him, will be a woman who calls "who is it" with a voice heavy with emotion when she's read a letter from him in which he disparages her manner of speech. This was a woman unmoved, a woman who cares not a whit for letters from unrequited lovers, disparaging or otherwise.

"Anthony Boisjoly," I replied, and was invited in.

Rosalind was in a chair by the high window which gave onto the garden. This was the Rose Room, and the hue of the walls and bedding reflected in the afternoon sun to bathe her in a pink glow. She was dressed in white cotton lace, and her hair was freely cascading over her shoulders. Rosalind was of the sort of natural beauty that transcends setting or situation — a delight to behold when soaking wet under cloudy skies, or crying beside a grave, or eating soup. That sort of beauty, operating with the advantage of lace, languishing hair, and a rosy radiance, beggars the word. Captivated by the moment, I confess that I forgot why I had come, and that I knew a man named Fiddles.

Gradually the rest of the scene came into focus, and the tea-table at Rosalind's side crystalised from a distracting blur into the belter which turns the tide of the game. On the table, on a silver tray, was an envelope, unopened and addressed, simply, 'Rosalind Pierpoint, Canterfell Hall'. She hadn't yet read the letter. This development caused me to reshape my immediate plans, and it explained why Rosalind was smiling in the sunlight, like one unaware that her accent had been slandered by the man who claimed to love her to all distraction.

"Hello, Mister Boisjoly," she said. "How very nice to see you."

This opening salvo, innocent as it was clearly meant, put me on the back foot. I realised in an instant that I had prepared no pretext for visiting Rosalind in her room, and had instead focused entirely on a strategy for trivialising the smear campaign of which I'd assumed she was aware.

"Yes," I said, struggling. "Lovely day."

Rosalind glanced out the window to verify my findings.

"Yes," she agreed. "Very."

An Englishman has never fully exhausted the subject of the weather, but I felt I should direct the momentum down a more fruitful path.

"Thought you'd like to know," I said. "Fiddles has gone with the police. Helping them with their enquiries."

"He's helping the police?"

"Yes," I said. "Quite normal. He's a trained barrister, you know, and a keen mind. They probably just want his views on some finer points of law."

"I expect that's what this note is about," she said, picking up the envelope.

"Oh, I don't think so," I said. "Probably not even from Fiddles."

"Who else would it be from?"

"Probably just a circular," I said. "Doubtless it'll be a promotion for a discount on washing powder. I'd discard it, were I you."

"A circular?" she said, looking at the envelope from either side. "Addressed to me?"

"Oh, yes," I said. "Unsolicited mail is a plague on the nation."

"Well, I certainly hope so. It would be very awkward if it were from Fairfax."

"Awkward?" I said. "Why awkward?"

"We had something of a tiff last night," she said. "I was afraid that this was his apology, and I don't know that I'm prepared to hear it."

"I admire that, you know. It's one of the many qualities of the American character that I think we British would do well to emulate. You don't shilly-shally about with letters and bottles of perfume, you act! A man forgets he owes you twenty dollars or whatever a reasonable amount might be, you don't wait for him to realise his mistake and stand you a round, you put your lawyers onto him. I like it, and I don't care who knows it. And now you're going to tear up that note and strike another blow for the New World over a decaying empire. Shall I do it for you?"

She was examining the note with a sort of quizzical look, and it was clear that my words had not penetrated. She took the envelope in both hands. She slipped a thumb into the flap. She snapped it open. She pinched the note and pulled it out. She unfolded it. She looked down at it. She said, "Could you hand me my glasses?"

I blinked at her, and I believe I may have in the same moment realised that I had been holding my breath.

"Your glasses?" I said.

"There, on the mantelpiece."

I turned to the fireplace. The shelf above it was a clutter of the hardware that women use to keep their hair and hips where the world expects to see them, and amongst the chaos was a thin and stylish pair of reading glasses, with encouragingly thick lenses. I affected to sort through the rubble, and with a daring sleight of hand I slipped the glasses into my pocket.

"No," I said, tentatively. "No, I don't see any glasses here."

"What a nuisance," she said. "I must have left them in the conservatory."

"Doubtless. Shall we go have a look for them?" I said, without a real plan, apart from separating Rosalind from the poison pen.

"No," she said. "I'm sure it's nothing."

"Quite so," I agreed, with considerable relief.

"You can read it to me."

"I wouldn't presume," I said.

"It's quite alright," she said. "Just look and see if it's an apology from Fairfax. If it is you can just tear it up for me."

I took the letter from her and glanced at it. It was as ripe as a fallen apple, and peppered with abusives like 'vulgar', 'vapid', 'insipid', and two uses of the word 'vacuous'. He had been modest with me when he described the letter as expressive — it was a chef d'oeuvre of defamation of Rosalind's accent, demeanour, manners, conversational skills and general intelligence. I only had a moment to take it in, but he appeared to be particularly expansive on the subject of her concept of fair play.

"It's an apology," I said. "Quite heartfelt, I'd say at a glance. I'll just dispose of it for you."

"No." Rosalind put a meditative finger to a pensive chin, and looked with musing eyes on the reflective sky. "I suppose I should hear it."

"Quite sure?" I asked. "Surely you don't want to endanger your reputation as a woman of resolve."

"Quite sure, Mister Boisjoly," she said, and looked at me with round eyes, reminiscent of a baby doe.

"Very well." I scanned the letter again, and settled on a policy of reversing almost everything in it. "My dearest Rosalind. Please accept my apologies for my behaviour this evening. I richly deserved your vitriolic response..."

"What is that word, Mister Boisjoly — vitriolic?"

"It means ladylike, I believe, in this context."

"Ah. Please continue."

"...your vitriolic response. I blame a cultural difference, and your, ehm, I think the word is 'admirably', yes, admirably bold manner of expressing yourself. My intrusions into your schooling and family were intended as casual conversation, and fully warranted the, ehm, charmingly idiomatic vindictive you employed." Here Fiddles had withdrawn his interest in knowing if they had common acquaintances in America, because to the best of his recollection he had associated with no baboons while there. I felt justified in extemporising based on what Fiddles had told me about his travels in the Atlantic states.

"My intrusive inquisitiveness," I continued on Fiddles' behalf, "was born of the pleasant memories I harbour of your home state, and the fine and entirely comprehensible people I encountered on the majestic Appalachian Trail, by the tranquil waters of Moosehead Lake and the churning seas of Fundy Bay..." I was hitting my stride, now, and giving a very good account of Fiddles' gift for painting a word-picture, "...and the generous beaches of Cape Cod."

"And what was that word, Mister Boisjoly?" asked Rosalind, engrossed now by Fiddles' heartfelt and evocative apology. In that instant, though, I realised that I had been indulging in free verse, like the agitators at Speakers' Corner, and I had no memory of what it was that I had just said.

"Word?" I equivocated. "Which one? I said rather a lot. Or rather, Fiddles does."

"The something something I employed," said Rosalind.

I referred to the letter. I had almost certainly been translating the phrase, 'vacuous vernacular that trips so naturally off your tongue'.

"Idiomatic verse?" I guessed.

"No, that wasn't it," she said, without conviction.

"I think it was," I said.

"That's actually quite poetic, isn't it?" she said, and then spoke "idiomatic verse" as though recalling a gem by Browning. "Please, go on, Mister Boisjoly."

"That's it, actually," I said, finally learning when to cut my losses. "It ends there. Yours truly, Fiddles. I mean Fairfax. Yours truly, Fairfax."

I took up the envelope and turned to the mantelpiece.

"I'll just leave it here for you, shall I?" I said, putting the empty envelope on the mantelpiece and the letter in my pocket. I lingered over the task of posing the envelope, and employed it as an illusionist employs deflection to return the reading glasses to the general disarray.

At that moment a timid tapping drew our attention. Luna was at the door, which I had left open, as a gentleman would.

"Miss," said Luna. "Your car is here."

"Car?" I said.

"I'm going to visit the village," said Rosalind. "So I called for a car."

"Oh, a car," I said. "It's a pleasant walk, you know. Just around the forest. Watch out for hunters, though. I'm led to understand that they're mostly down from London, these days, and make few fine distinctions when selecting their target."

"That sounds delightful," enthused Rosalind. "Will you join me? You won't mind carrying some of my equipment." She gestured to a collection of cases and canisters leaning neatly in the corner of the room.

"Going fishing?" I asked. "The river trout will bite your hand off for live flies, and I can tell you where to get all those you like."

"It's a camera," she explained. "I'm going to take some pictures of the church."

"Saint George's," I said. "An excellent choice. It's Norman. From eleven hundred and twenty. The roof, however, dates from a funding drive during the war. I put up five pounds. My name is on a plaque behind the baptismal font, which can be seen anytime, day or night, because the funding drive failed to extend to replacing the church door."

"It sounds delightful," said Rosalind. "I was going to go yesterday, but I thought that might be received as disrespectful, in view of everything that happened."

"Quite right, too," I said. "Twenty-four hours is the standard moratorium on still-life after a murder in England. What is it back home?"

"I don't know." Rosalind took on a demeanour of puzzled disquiet, the way a puppy looks when you pretend to throw a stick. "I don't think it's ever come up."

"I think you'd best take the car," I said. "The church is a full goat-stench from here, and I should really stick on. The clock is rather ticking on getting to the bottom of this murder."

"Ticking? Why is the clock ticking?"

"Oh, you know," I said. "What with one thing and another, clocks will go on ticking, what?"

"I see. Well, thank you, Mister Boisjoly," said Rosalind. She'd returned to looking idly out the window. "You must tell Fairfax to come and see me when he's done helping the police."

Luna and I shifted the camera gear to the waiting taxi, the driver of which watched helpfully from the front seat, smoking a cigarette. I then accompanied the maid back to the tradesman's entrance, by way of the south lawn.

"Breakfast was a delight this morning, Luna," I said, in an expressly off-hand tone.

"Thank you, sir," she said, and then quickly edited, "I'll be sure to tell Miss Lively."

"Will she be lucid at this hour?" I asked.

"I don't know what you mean, sir," said Luna to her fingers, which twiddled an energetic reply.

"Of course you do, Luna," I said. "Miss Lively is no cook. Her talents, prodigious as they may be, lie elsewhere — outdrinking career sailors, for instance — but I've only tasted black pudding congealed to such a fine crust by two other chefs, one of whom has a royal appointment, just for black pudding and toad in the hole."

"Miss Lively's head of kitchen," explained Luna to a particularly attentive thumb. "She prepares all the meals."

"I'll give you the bacon," I said, munificently, "but the black pudding was patently not the work of a woman who thinks boiled sherry is a passable stand-in for consommé."

Luna had no reply for this, and her fingers twiddled disconsolately.

"I find myself wondering where she got her training," I continued, musing. "Holloway Prison for Women, do you think? Or a tannery?"

"Miss Lively's never been outside of Fray, Mister Boisjoly," said Luna earnestly.

"She must have been at some point, Luna," I assured her. "She told me that she's worked in great houses all her life, and there's only one great house in Fray."

"She's never set foot outside the town, she says," insisted Luna, "and very proud of it, too."

"Very prudent of her," I said. "Most of the outside world is just a thin reflection of the majestic shadow cast by the metropolis of Fray. Talking of the migratory patterns of the English Lively, where was she while you were preparing breakfast yesterday?"

Luna returned to keeping council with her hands. "Miss Lively often has strong headaches in the mornings, sir. They keep her in bed sometimes until quite late."

"I don't wonder she does," I said. "I suffer a similar affliction myself, usually on mornings following boat race night."

We arrived at the kitchen door and there we paused. I had learned what I needed to learn with regards to the exotic and enigmatic Dorothea Lively, but it seemed a waste to simply slam shut the flood gates now they'd been opened. I endeavoured to balance out another mystery that had been playing on my mind.

"I say, this Lydde chap," I said, choosing my words delicately. "Rather a clammy bit of ooze, isn't he?"

Luna drew herself to her full height and looked me square in the tie clip. "I don't know what you mean, sir," she said.

"Well, that's nice to hear," I said. "I have the very strong impression, Luna, that he feels the same way about you."

"My relationship with Mister Lydde is quite proper, sir."

"Of that I have no doubt," I assured her. "The man has all the romance of Euclidian division."

"He's very ideal and logical, is all."

"Do you mean ideological?" I asked. "I concur. Hard luck for him to have to apply all that higher vision to butlering. I'm sure he'd be much more in his element storming winter palaces and assuming the means of production."

"He just wants taking in hand, sir," said Luna.

"You're right, Luna," I said. "And I think you're just the woman to do it."

CHAPTER THIRTEEN
The Inscrutable Nature of the English Summer

A clear English sky and a simmering Sussex sun can cohabitate peacefully for only so long. Temperatures can only rise so high. Pressures develop between opposing fronts. It's not long before things have become positively precipitous.

And so it was that the skies of Fray grew cluttered with ill-minded clouds, approaching from all points and converging as of the braids of an ashen veil directly over Canterfell Hall. There they lingered, rumbling abuse at one another, spoiling for a brawl. The invective grew in volume and affront, and in due season something was said which could not be taken back. The tempest was unleashed upon the earth, as though on the orders of a jealous God who'd only just noticed that it'd been a while since his fool-hardy creation had had its last ticking off.

I witnessed this positioning of forces within the cosmic arena from the comfort and isolation of a deep leather armchair in the conservatory. The effect was much like the dimming of the cinema lights before the main feature. All was purple stillness. Then the production exploded onto the screen in a furious spectacle of flickering lightning and lashing rain, drumming on the glass roof of the conservatory with an unnerving urgency.

The thrum and drama were somehow censorious, as though nature's elements had found common cause and, if they could just get past the vaulted roof of iron and glass, they'd dish me a well-deserved pounding. The facts are laid before you, boomed the thunder. You need only get them in the right order, elucidated the lightning. So get on with it, repeated the rain in a looping chorus, you posing great stick.

Trenchant, but fair, although I think the rain overstated the point, rather. I set my mind to the conundrum, spread before me like a jigsaw puzzle. The pieces were all there — the location of everyone at the time of the murder, the unique disposition of the castle, which converges the drawing-room, the wings, and the tower onto the main entrance, the curious comportment of all concerned since the murder, and the stated views that each held with respect to the deceased. I had the false testimony of the major, Laetitia, and Lively, and the presumably honest report of Fiddles, Vickers, Hal, Rosalind, Lydde, and Mallet. There were the conflicting chronicles of the codicil, an intrigue in itself, and the surprise late entry, an earldom in abeyance.

And it came to me. The clouds cleared — metaphorically, of course, the real things were still thick as thieves and causing all manner of mischief overhead — the bits and snippets took form, jostling for position and clicking into place and leading me inexorably to...

"Cocktails, Mister Boisjoly."

And it was gone, to be replaced by the baffled countenance of Vickers. He had about him the air of dazed accomplishment of one whose longshot, chosen on the strength of its silks, has just placed at nineteen-to-one."

"For pity's sake, man," I protested. "Is that how you announce cocktails, or anything short of the outbreak of war, to a man on the cusp of a revelation? It's a good job you weren't on hand when it was time for tea in the Einstein household, or we'd all still be completely in the dark regarding the disposition of E with respect to MC squared."

"I beg your pardon, sir," he said. His face fell back into the studied tapestry of wrinkled insensitivity by which Vickers is widely known. "I was unaware that you were engaged in thought."

I regretted my reaction the moment I'd had it. Lone footmen in their golden years, I expect, have few enough moments of triumph as a share of their daily routine, and here I'd dashed to the ground the simple victory the man had enjoyed in the rare act of recognising someone from the past.

"My fault," I said. "Doubtless it'll come back to me. Let us salvage what we can from this affair, Vickers, were you whooping something about cocktails?"

"Yes, sir," he said. "I've been asked to inform you that refreshments are served in the drawing-room, and that a fire has been lit in the main hall."

These two developments would have been received as well-enunciated non-sequiturs to anyone unfamiliar with Canterfell Hall, but to those of us who'd sought refuge there from storms past, these words glowed with nostalgic comfort. Indeed, in the hour or so I'd been lingering in the conservatory, watching the weather make and execute its divine plan, the temperature had dropped to a bone-chilling reminder that, summer or not, this was still England. The conservatory was at the end of the new wing and formed of glass and, consequently, impervious to all efforts to provide heating. But a roaring fire in the great ornate kiln in the main hall meant dry, soft, enveloping warmth through the drawing-room and as far as the dining room.

"Rush on ahead, Vickers," I said. "Make mine a warm brandy."

Passing through the main hall I confirmed that there was a roaring conflagration in the fireplace. A great fire in a great hall is a great thing to behold, but when it's the only source of heat and light in a medieval castle at the centre of a belting storm, it takes on romantic properties, like rowing on the Serpentine on a sunny afternoon, or being twelve years old.

The effect is universal, and it exerts itself even on Americans, apparently, for transfixed before the fire was the figure of Rosalind. She appeared to be wearing something tenaciously clingy, so that she rendered a daring silhouette against the orange flame. I felt like an intruder and some reflex, instilled in my subconscious by a dogmatic nanny or high-minded housemaster, impelled me to announce my presence.

"Coming in for a bracer, Miss Pierpoint?"

She turned, then, and drove home with passion the point I believe I made earlier about a beauty which conquers all conditions. Rosalind was a delight to the eye, not in spite of but because she was soaking wet. Her hair stuck to her face in ropes that somehow looked like what everyone would be doing with their hair next season. Her silk gown had been transformed into something resembling a wet sail, and she wore it the way they'll be wearing wet sails on Paris runways when they show the autumn collection. Makeup ran down her face in black rivulets, in the manner of Cézanne's Dark

Period. Her lips curled down at the corners and she shivered with a delicate charm.

"It's raining," she said wanly, as one who has been gravely disappointed by a meteorological system with whom she felt she had an understanding.

"So I see," I said. "What you want is dry clothes and warm brandy. And then some more warm brandy. In that order. Can I be of some assistance?"

"Luna is bringing me a towel."

"Ah, then I'll leave you to the loosening of whalebone and unclipping of clasps," I said. "We're gathering in the drawing-room, when you're ready."

And so we were. I was particularly relieved to lay eyes on Fiddles, who seemed no worse for what must have been a daring escape. He was installed at the filling station, busying himself with a chafing dish and brandy snifters the size of goldfish bowls. Hal and Laetitia were fully equipped with simmering goblets of the fuel of French philosophy, and the air was heady with the unmistakable perfume of quality brandy, warmed to something between ninety-nine and a hundred and one degrees. This was to be expected, though, but a late addition to the programme included Halliwell Canterfell and List Porter, understudying the roles of bewildered spectator and surprise guest, respectively.

"Hello Mister Canterfell, Porter," I said with genuine pleasure at the encounter. "What brings you to Canterfell Hall?"

"I accompanied Mister Canterfell," said Porter. "On account of the rain. And I have remained, at the kind invitation of Mister Canterfell, on account of the bridge being flooded."

"And I've come, against my better judgement," said the

honourable member, "because some odious chief-inspector tells me that Fairfax is under suspicion of having murdered Sebastian. And I needed some shirts."

The party atmosphere of a well-equipped castle under siege of a summer storm was further complemented by Luna, delivering new glassware, and Vickers, bringing fresh spirit.

"I think that Miss Pierpoint is standing gamely by for that warm towel," I reminded Luna. "You'll find her shivering in a most lady-like manner before the fire in the main hall."

"Yes, Mister Boisjoly," said Luna to a stubborn blemish on the toe of my shoe, and sped off, presumably, to a linen closet somewhere above stairs.

"This must be some sort of record," I said to Fiddles, as he handed me a steaming bowl of Cognac. "Hug always insisted that we keep his company until at least sun-up, if memory serves, even under caution for the trifling offence of being drunk in charge of a cow."

"Pre-trial custody is at the discretion of the arresting officer, should he judge there to be risk of flight or interference in an ongoing investigation," explained Fiddles. "And if you'll recall, in that instance the animal in question needed rescuing from the roof of the Mason Hall."

"Hug had no such reservations on this occasion?" I asked.

"I explained that in the absence of cause, under the Habeas Corpus Act of 1679 the accused has absolute right of bail," said Fiddles. "I didn't have anything on me, it turns out, so Hug and I settled on the three pounds six he owed me for a bet I placed on his behalf on a sentimental favourite in the half-term all-girls steeplechase."

"It's bail, then is it?" I said into the cavern of my snifter. "I was hoping that Inspector Wittersham had seen the error of his ways."

"No such luck," said Fiddles, shaking his head despairingly. "I'm confined to the castle. They escorted me here, in fact. Lydde's dropping them back in town now. How have you made out, Anty? Have you sorted out who did it yet? If you'll allow me a moment of self-indulgence, I don't much fancy the idea of hanging."

"Very nearly there, Fiddles old man, no need to go to pieces."

"Of course, forgive me."

"Quite understandable," I assured him. "Out of simple curiosity, though, how much time would you say that I have to do the inspector's job for him?"

I probably should have pulled the emergency brake on that damning indictment of the forces of law and order the moment I heard the door open behind me, but some mechanism deep in my subconscious, responsible for balancing probabilities, assured me that the odds of Ivor being present were negligible. So of course there he was, with Hug at his side.

"I'd say that you ran out the clock this morning," answered the inspector. "Mister Canterfell will be taken to London tomorrow for arraignment. This time, he won't be coming back."

Ivor and Hug were handing wet cloaks and coats and helmets and hats to Lydde, who took them with a glad camaraderie with his fellow working-class enemies of privilege. All three men displayed the apportioned, top-story dampness that comes from passing from car to house in the pouring rain.

"What a pleasure," I said. "I surmise that you have returned owing to the rain having rendered the bridge impassable."

"Never seen it so bad," said Hug. "Not since they dredged the river to build the mill."

"We owe the weather a debt of gratitude," I said. "Fiddles, two more hot brandies for the inspector and Hug whom, I think we can say at this hour, are no longer bound by the restrictions of duty."

"I'll do one for Hug," said Fiddles, petulantly. "But the inspector can have his cold."

"Come along, Fiddles, that's hardly the Oxford rowing team spirit," I said. "And in any case I feel very strongly that before this evening ends you and the inspector will have fallen on each other's necks as brothers."

"Brothers, you say," scoffed Fiddles, with the artless irony of the men who read Law at school.

"Reunited brothers," I said, doubling down, "who've done one another a profound disservice."

The door opened then and Rosalind came in, followed by Luna. Rosalind had put the damp past behind her and now appeared to have just come from hair and makeup and was ready for her closeup. She smiled with delight at the festive gathering, as might a child at the centre of a milestone birthday party. Say, her tenth.

Feet were rapidly leapt to, salutations were hastily exchanged, and Cognac was worked up to drinking temperature. Luna and Lydde stood either side of the door to the dining room, casting each other awkward glances. Vickers stood by the drinks cabinet, squinting at all the new faces. Ivor, Hug and Porter occupied an amorphous no-man's land between servant and served. The honourable member was splayed on an embroidered divan like a discarded marionette, his feet up on a spindly, Victorian-style side-table which was ill-suited to the purpose. Laetitia and Hal sat in a corner, beneath portraits of Hal's ancestors, who peered down on them with forbearance. Fiddles was rotating snifters over the chafing dish.

It should all have been very chummy, what with the brandy and the thunder rumbling all around us and the fire crackling in the main hall, but there was a decided undercurrent of remoteness to the assembly. Except for Rosalind, who appeared to be playing some sort of guessing game of her own invention, everyone appeared content to keep their own company until the waters receded.

"Is there any enthusiasm for a rousing round of Minister's Cat?" I asked no one and everyone.

"That sounds delightful," said Rosalind. "What is it?"

"It's a singing game," I explained, "in which all participants cast aspersions on the character of the vicar's moggie, in alphabetical order."

"It sounds hard," complained Rosalind.

"It is," I agreed. "It's been largely abandoned in better society on account of being too cerebral. How about, Are You There Moriarity?"

"It's hardly the appropriate time for parlour games, Mister Boisjoly," said Ivor.

"Quite right," I agreed. "We've got two policemen, a mysterious death, and a dark and stormy night. How about instead we solve a murder?"

"Rather a redundant exercise," said Ivor, "considering it's already been solved."

"Indulge me, Inspector. I think I can surprise you," I said. "Your view is that my dear friend Fiddles killed his uncle, and the motive was the earldom?"

"The motive was power," corrected Ivor. "With the peerage redirected to his family line, when the major dies

Mister Halliwell Canterfell would inherit the title, and move to the House of Lords, allowing Mister Fairfax to stand for his seat in parliament and, one day, becoming Lord Canterfell himself."

"Lord Bunce, Earl of Fray" corrected Fiddles, "to give the title its correct styling."

"Very well, Lord Bunce," conceded Ivor. "It's still motive for murder. Not to mention the wealth and prestige that comes with being a peer."

"Prestige, Inspector," said Fiddles. "The earldom has no property, and hasn't since it was put in abeyance five hundred years ago."

"I concede the point," said Ivor handsomely. "You only killed your uncle for prestige and power, not wealth."

"But your case pivots on delicate timing," I said. "We are in agreement that whoever killed Sebastian Canterfell was in the gallery at the time of the murder."

"And the only person that could have been, by Mister Fairfax's own testimony, was himself," said Ivor.

"And the killer."

"Redundant point," said Ivor. "Everyone else can account for their whereabouts. Mallet saw Vickers in the conservatory and Mister Harold in the terrace sunroom. Mister Harold accounts for Miss Pierpoint and Miss Pierpoint accounts for Lydde. Mrs Canterfell and the major were together. The maid was doing the linen. Porter and Mister Halliwell were at the Hare's Foot."

Well, exactly, Inspector," I said. "That's not everyone."

"It's everyone with a motive," he said. "Mrs Canterfell, we can assume, might have wanted her husband out of the way for romantic reasons. Lydde here might have thought he was striking a blow for the working man. Mister Harold could have wanted to assume his father's role as manager of the vast estate. Mister Halliwell might have wanted the title for himself or his son. But they were all elsewhere when the murder was committed."

"I beg to differ, Inspector," I said. "What about Miss Lively?"

"What about her?"

"Did you ask her where she was at the time of the death of Sebastian Canterfell?"

"She was clearing up the kitchen after breakfast," said Ivor. "And she has no motive to kill her employer."

"On the contrary, Inspector, in fact on two contraries. Dorothea Lively had every reason to kill Sebastian Canterfell."

This declaration was accompanied by a flawlessly timed clap of thunder, and all eyes fell on me.

"Well?" said Ivor.

"You'll recall the story of Dottie and Jules?" I said. "The years have not been kind to her, but Dorothea Lively and Dottie the upstairs maid are one and the same."

"How do you come to know that?" asked Fiddles.

"She told me herself," I said, "when she claimed to have always worked in great houses. She only overlooked mentioning that it was always the same great house — Canterfell Hall. She fell on difficult times after her young suitor, the only real love of her life, was sent packing back to Normandy by the austerity measures imposed by Sebastian Canterfell."

"So she's not a cook at all?" said Fiddles. "Well, that certainly explains the suet pudding."

"But it does not explain breakfast," I declared. "Because Miss Lively addressed the problem of a broken romance with the all-too-common remedy of repeated and generous applications of cooking sherry. She doesn't prepare breakfast, because she never gets up before noon, leaving Luna to practice her secret passion and talent for kippers and blood pudding."

"Is this true, Luna?" said Fiddles.

The sparrow dressed as a maid shivered on the spot, and in time the shaking reached her extremities, and manifested as a brisk nod of the head.

"Fine," said Ivor. "Miss Lively had cause to commit murder, but as you say she was in bed with a hangover at the time of the death of Sebastian Canterfell."

"Indeed," I agreed. "I merely present the case of Miss Lively as an object lesson. She didn't kill Sebastian Canterfell, but you didn't know that she had a motive, just as you didn't know that someone else who did have a motive, someone in this very room with us now, could not account for his whereabouts at the time of the murder."

"I think we've covered everyone, Mister Boisjoly," said Hug, his hand hovering over his notepad, like a wild west gunslinger, awaiting the high-noon bell or whatever it is sets those people off.

"You haven't got quite everyone," I said. I scanned the anxious faces of the room. All looked at me with anticipation and then at their neighbour with furtive suspicion. Hug, Ivor, Hal, Laetitia, Lydde, Luna, Porter, Halliwell, Fiddles — each face registered anxiety and apprehension. Except for one.

"I say," I said. "Has anyone seen the major?"

"I saw him this evening," said Hal. "He was quite diffident."

"More so than usual?" asked Fiddles.

"Oh, rather," said Hal. "I tried to draw him out regarding

the time he was shot in Mandalay, and he said, uncannily, that he couldn't recall the occasion."

"Couldn't recall one of his stories," said Fiddles. "Are you quite sure you weren't talking to Vickers here? No offence, Vickers."

"None taken, sir."

"I spoke to him this afternoon," said Laetitia, distractedly. "I may have struck an emotional chord with him, regarding certain private confidences."

"Has anyone seen him since?" I asked.

"When I saw him he said that he was heading to the gallery, to sort out a few things," said Hal.

In the next moment a terrible explosion shook the medieval foundations of the castle. It wasn't thunder — it was too loud and too close and too inside Canterfell Hall to have been thunder — it was a gunshot. A gunshot indoors is quite a singular affair, so different in degree from the discharge of a gun in the woods as to be different in kind. The impact is like a physical thing, that comes right up to you, claps you on both ears, and shouts "Someone's been shot!"

Hug led the way, with Ivor in close pursuit, out the drawing-room doors and up the tower stairs. The crack still echoed as we dashed up and stopped, in some silent mutual understanding, at the gallery door. It was locked. Hug bounced his soft bulk against the sturdy oak several times, then bent to peer through the keyhole. He turned to us — I was at the landing with Hal and Fiddles behind me on the stairs — his look of bleached dread described everything he'd seen. Ivor pushed him aside and looked through the keyhole. Then he stood, put his hands on his hips and shook his head and, I fancy, regretted his choice of trade.

CHAPTER FOURTEEN
The Frightful Fate of the Fourth Earl of Fray

Lydde was sent for the key and there was no difficulty unlocking the door. Ivor and Hug entered the gallery, closely followed by Fiddles, Hal, and Halliwell. I recruited Lydde in a sweep of the rest of the tower. We moved up the stairs to the study, which was empty, and then climbed out onto the ramparts. There was no one, of course, and Lydde and I looked at each other in the driving rain, with the fraternal acknowledgement mad dogs and Englishmen are said to exchange when meeting under the midday sun. We drained back inside and reported to the first floor, where the disposition of the major, vis-a-vis life, was largely as expected.

Fiddles and his father looked down at the body of their grandfather and father respectively. Hal, overcome, dashed from the room, but not before taking a moment to collide with the door frame, which inspired Ivor to order from the room everyone who was not an officer of the law.

The mob cleared to reveal the decidedly Gothic triptych of a dead soldier with a policeman on either side, his trophies aligned on opposing image planes, composed on a vanishing point at the centre of an open window, beyond which a storm crackled and roared. The rain blew through the window in sheets, and the floor was fully flooded with water and blood, which glimmered in the light from the landing. Ivor looked at me, then, and appeared to fix me with glowering accusation, and in that same moment a flash of white lightning lit his ashen face.

"The major has been shot," announced Ivor. He was standing at the drawing-room door, addressing what most theatre people would recognise instantly as a 'tough audience'. "It would appear to be a case of suicide."

"Nonsense," protested Hal. "The major would sooner shoot you than himself."

"Nevertheless," persisted Ivor, "that is the state of affairs. Mister Lydde, are there any other keys to the gallery?"

Lydde explained that he didn't even know that there were two, and so to the best of his knowledge the inspector was in possession of all known copies.

"Very well then," said Ivor. "We'll get to the bottom of this in the morning. In the meantime the gallery will remain locked, and I'm afraid that the scene cannot be disturbed."

"You don't propose leaving the major like that all night, Inspector," protested Hal.

"The body has been covered, Mister Canterfell," said Hug, with the firmly reassuring tone they teach at community constable college. "And we've closed the window, so he'll be quite comfortable."

"You're all familiar with the process by now, I think," announced Ivor with a withering tone. "We'll start with you,

Mrs Canterfell, and one by one take your statement in the conservatory." He opened the door by way of invitation. "Next will be Miss Pierpoint, so that we might allow the ladies to retire, but I would ask each of you to refrain from discussing what you saw or heard until after you've spoken to myself and Constable Pennybun, after which I would ask you all to keep to your rooms until tomorrow morning."

Mrs Canterfell, walking in a daze, accompanied Ivor and Hug to the conservatory, and Fiddles set about warming up more brandy.

"What an extraordinary thing," said Hal. "How was it done, Anty?"

"How was what done?" I asked.

"Well, it's another locked-room mystery, isn't it?" he said. "Grandpapa did not kill himself, and yet we all heard the shot, and there was no one else in the tower."

"I think we'd be well-advised to respect the inspector's request to not discuss our statements prior to making them," said Fiddles, distributing drinks. "And in any case there's a more pressing matter to be addressed. Everyone got a drink? Good."

Fiddles took the floor in the middle of the room and faced his father, who had returned to the embroidered divan and was amusing himself with a loose thread.

"Lady and gentlemen," said Fiddles. "I give you the Right Honourable Lord Bunce, Fourth Earl of Fray."

There was slight delayed reaction, not long, but momentous, in the juxtaposition between a Halliwell at repose, delighting in an errant bit of thread, and an honoured member of the peerage, spasming from the news as though it had come to him in the form of a hat pin to the thigh.

"Good God, you're right," said the right honourable member, leaping to his feet. "Fairfax, I'm meant to be addressing parliament on Monday. You must do something — it's the first reading of my bill to legislate an annual badger census."

"I think it may have to wait," said Fiddles. "Members of the peerage cannot sit in parliament, you know that."

"I'll renounce."

"You can't renounce your title."

"Why not?" said Halliwell. "You're a barrister. We have witnesses, all of sound mind and reputation."

Fiddles fixed Hal and myself with silent, weary calls for support.

"Why not, Fairfax?" said Hal. "It's going to come to you anyway."

"I have to agree, Fiddles." I said. "If the honourable member is determined, I see no reason to deprive the country of a fuller understanding of the domestic makeup of the national badger population, just to stand on ceremony."

"What's going on?" sang Rosalind.

"Fairfax is going to become an earl," I explained. "Right now, before our very eyes."

"How exciting," said Rosalind. "Will we meet the king?"

"I'm not going to become an earl, not now, at any rate," said Fiddles.

"Oh, please, Fairfax," said Rosalind, with a tone of newfound admiration. "I want to meet the king."

"You can't renounce your title, Father, because titles can't be renounced," explained Fiddles.

"That's absurd," said Halliwell. "They can't force a man to accept a title he doesn't want."

"I'm afraid that they can, Father," said Fiddles. "There is

no mechanism in law to refuse a title."

"But there's a mechanism to be disqualified for this one, isn't there Fairfax?" asked Hal.

"What do you mean?" said Fiddles. "Of course not."

"No, I'm quite sure you told me that there was a... splendid reminder? Or some such antiquated expression, associated with the letters patent."

"No," said Fiddles, squinting into the middle distance, as though seeking far afield that which he knows perfectly well is in his back pocket. "No, I don't think so."

"Of course. You know, Mister Fairfax," injected Porter. "The Special Remainder."

"That's it, a Special Remainder," agreed Hal. "What about that?"

"I don't quite see how that applies, Hal," said Fiddles, with subtle menace, as though just stopping short of adding 'now shut your pie-hole'.

"Ah, well," said Hal, like a man who's just realised that he's worn a white tie to a funeral. "My mistake. Withdrawn."

"What's this, Fairfax?" said the honourable member. "Is there a Special Remainder attached to the Letters Patent?"

"Quick preliminary question, Fiddles," I said. "What are we talking about? What are Letters Patent, and what is special about their remainder?"

"The Letters Patent formed the original decree setting out the earldom of Fray," said Fiddles. "Sometime early in the reign of Charles II they were amended with a Special Remainder, a sort of addendum that the crown sometimes employs when a title can't find its own way along the line of succession."

"What does it do?" I asked, feeling like one playing Twenty Questions to the rules of Hunt the Thimble.

"I'm not quite sure that I recall, exactly," said Fiddles, running his finger around the rim of his snifter, but appearing to gain little satisfaction from the exercise.

"Begging your pardon, Mister Fairfax, it qualifies the petitioner," said Porter. "The earldom was in abeyance, owing to a small matter of treason, when Charles II, wary of what become of his poor father at the hands of them he probably thought of as friends, used a Special Remainder to deny the restoration of the earldom to anyone unwilling to swear allegiance to the House of Stuart."

"Usurpers!" declared the honourable member.

"Yes, thank you Porter," said Fiddles, dismissively.

"Your Special Remainders, as a rule," continued Porter, casting about for an audience and settling on me, "confer titles on nephews or cousins, allowing a title to continue, even if there ain't no one to inherit, or skipping a generation, should the rightful heir turn out to be simple, or German."

"But this Special Remainder is, for lack of a less tautological word, special," I said.

"T'is. Being that the earldom was in abeyance, the Special Remainder added a condition — the title could be restored to the petitioner, qualified by the law of progenation, who signed his allegiance to the royal house of the day."

"The Stuarts," I said.

"The Stuarts," confirmed Porter.

"How do you come to know all this?" I asked, but then thought better of it, "In fact, Porter, save that story for another stormy night. Does this mean that Mister Halliwell needs only refuse to sign an oath to a dormant royal name, and he can remain in parliament?"

"Yes, sir," said Porter. "He would keep his seat until the next election, when he would be run out of town pursued, in all probability, by dogs."

"Dogs, you say."

"Dogs, sir," said Porter with admirable self-composure, given the company. "The village is very much partial to the earldom, and would be quite aggrieved were it to remain in abeyance."

"Would it remain in abeyance?" I asked.

"It would," said Porter, solemnly. "Until such time as the passing of Mister Canterfell." Porter paused a moment, now, and inclined his head to the honourable member. "God rest your soul, sir."

"Well there you go, Father," said Fiddles. "It's either the House of Lords or nothing, pursued by dogs."

"I shall never betray the House of Wessex," insisted Halliwell, standing proud and then, after doddering for a bit, returning to the divan. "You do it."

"Don't be an ass, Father."

"You could, Mister Fairfax," said Porter. "You'd just need to sign an oath of allegiance to the House of Stuart."

"I could," said Fairfax. "But I won't. I'm not retiring to the House of Lords at the age of twenty-nine."

"Of course, Fairfax, it's the ideal solution," said Halliwell, beaming at his son. "Me in parliament, you in the Lords, the British badger would finally have a voice in government."

Fiddles regarded his father beneath hooded eyes, and then turned his attention, by all outward appearances, to a tattered flag waving on a distant hill, obscured by the smoke and ash of glorious battle.

"Is this your final word, Father?" asked Fiddles, with a delivery that transported me body and soul to the Haymarket Theatre where I heard Barrymore lament "To be, or not to be..."

Fiddles sent Lydde for paper, pen, and ink, and presently he was writing a document that would not only weigh heavily on the affairs of the nation, but change the course of events for every badger in the land. Joy would ring out, too, across the fields and dales of Fray starting, no doubt, at the Hare's Foot Inn and Tavern.

The honourable member wasted no time signing his name as a witness, and he tapped his foot energetically until such time as Porter and I had done the same. Then, one by one, the party broke up as the membership kept their appointments with the forces of law and order.

"So, it's to be the House of Lords, Your Lordship," I said to Fiddles. We were the last to linger in the drawing-room.

"We're old friends, Anty," said Fiddles, offhandedly. "Call me Lord Bunce."

"You're not concerned how this will appear to the inspector?"

"It crossed my mind," he said. "But I received the impression that Inspector Wittersham is hell-bent that I should hang, regardless. I think I could dance on Uncle Sebastian's grave, at this point, and he'd be no more convinced of my guilt than he is now."

"Best not, if only for form's sake," I said. "It'll be hard enough keeping you from the gallows when Inspector Wittersham figures it out."

"Figures what out, Anty?" asked Fiddles, idly turning a snifter against the light of the chandelier.

"You know very well, what," I said. "That reluctant hero twaddle. You knew about this Special Remainder, and you knew that your father would insist that you assume the earldom and enter the House of Lords, where you'll never have to bother trying to win favour with the half-wit voting public of the village of Fray."

"That obvious, was it?"

"Oh, I don't know," I said, musing. "I suppose your plan to install yourself in the House of Lords might have been more apparent had you performed the role actually dressed in scarlet robes with collar of miniver pure, but of course, I know you. It may take the inspector, handicapped by a lack of familiarity with your overleaping ambition to meddle in the affairs of state, as much as half the morning to get to grips with the thing."

Straw was laid down in the Merigold, Pearl, and Yellow Rooms respectively for the guests, and after each of us had said and signed some variation of 'There I was in the drawing-room when I heard a gunshot,' we all went to bed. I don't know what others do when finding themselves in a strange bed in a great house rank with the stench of death, indeed, I'm not sure what I would do were it to become habit-forming, but on this night I lay awake, listening to the rain thrumming on my window. Others, doubtless, did likewise, but for one, for whom the night yet owed an adventure.

CHAPTER FIFTEEN
The Puzzling Case of the Puzzling Case

Breakfast was served on the sideboard in the dining room and Luna, apparently one of those anxious types for whom stress is a source of nervous energy, had baked a ham. There were also potatoes *au gratin*, a latticework of bacon, and some sort of desert *soufflé*. Raspberry, I think.

There was a silent unease in the atmosphere that could have been cut into blocks and used to build a sturdy shed. Hal and his mother sat at the head and corner of the table respectively, wide-eyed and still, like a formal portrait of a mother and son, captured at the instant they'd both been hit in the face with a salmon. Fiddles occupied himself with a cold cup of tea, and with alternating his attention between the clock on the wall, which reported a wholesome eight-fifteen, and the drinks cabinet. Ivor allowed himself a small portion of potato, which he ate standing up. Only Rosalind and the honourable member displayed any serious interest in breakfast, although they approached the subject with radically different plans of action. For Rosalind, the sideboard presented an array of exotic delights, a kickshaw of quaint delicacies from the heritage kitchens of the exotic isle of 'England'. Halliwell, meanwhile, piled his plate high and indiscriminately, and ate with a deliberate gluttony, as though collecting on a long overdue debt. Personally, I ate for duty's sake, and restored my tissues with two slices of ham, most of the bacon, potatoes, lashings of coffee, and *soufflé*, only so that I might be in form for the challenging day ahead. I had a strong premonition that things were about to unfold, and unfold quickly.

The door opened, roughly in lines with my premonition, and Hug appeared and said, "Inspector?"

"What is it, Constable?"

"I think you'd best come up the tower," said Hug.

Ivor paused his fork and looked skyward. "What now, Constable?"

"There's been a break-in."

"In the tower?" asked Ivor.

"In the gallery, sir," said Hug. "The lock has been forced."

"Has anything been disturbed?" asked Ivor, nevertheless abandoning his plate of potatoes to the sideboard.

"On close examination of the premises, sir," said Hug. "I would have to say... possibly."

"Possibly."

"It's very hard to say, sir," said Hug. "There are a lot of things in the gallery. I can't say if any of them are not."

"The major showed me the gallery yesterday," I said. "Perhaps I could be of service?"

"Oh, very well," said Ivor resignedly, as though the break-in, my participation and, shortly, a plague of locusts was all but inevitable. "Come along."

The door to the gallery had indeed been forced. Some flat-headed instrument, such as a jimmy bar that a burglar might employ for exactly this purpose, had been used to break the frame where it meets — or used to meet — the latchbolt. The floor was still wet, but the sun had been reconciled with its familiar blue habitat, and the landscape outside the window was once again its leafy, lush, English self.

The major was discreetly covered, from the shoulders up, by the Union Jack which had been on the wall, housing his medals. In his hand was the service revolver. The room appeared to be otherwise undisturbed, apart from the brass and rosewood box with a pyramid lid.

"The chest is missing," I said.

"What chest?" asked Ivor, with a tone that suggested that if there ever had been a chest, it was me that put it there.

"The major's box of intimate ammunition," I explained. "It's an ornate box, about the size of, well, a box, and it's got brass knobs and dials, by which one unlocks its secrets."

"I recall it now," said Ivor. "It had nothing in it but stones."

"Bullets and arrowheads, in fact," I said, "all of which share the unique distinction of at one time having been inside the major."

"Anything else?"

"No, I think that's it," I said, looking about the room, distracted not by what was missing, but by what was not.

"Anything else in the box, Mister Boisjoly," clarified Ivor with a withering tone. "You said it held secrets."

"I wouldn't be at all surprised," I said. "But I was only introduced to the missiles. They were quite dear to the man."

"Why would someone break in to steal that?" mused Ivor, in a manner which I probably should have recognised as rhetorical.

"Because the door was locked," I said. "The door is never locked, and it was only locked last night, exceptionally, on your command."

"How is that material to anything at all?" asked Ivor.

"I merely point out, Inspector, that if anyone had wanted access to this room, they would have to have broken in."

"That will be all, Mister Boisjoly," said Ivor.

"Might I just have a glance at the body, Inspector?" I asked. "I may be able to offer further insights."

"Your explanation of the need for a burglar to break down a locked door has already advanced the case enormously," said Ivor, with what I'm sure he felt was cutting irony. "We are much indebted to you, Mister Boisjoly, but you must let us perform at least some of the police work."

Whatever other criticisms might be reasonably levelled against your typical great house — they're notoriously difficult to heat in winter, for instance, and in my most recent experience they appeared to be absolute death traps — great houses tend to have in common the singular advantage of an abundance of house. This makes them among the ideal venues, along with the bath and vanity gallery openings, in which to be alone with one's thoughts, whether one likes the idea or not. This was especially so of Canterfell Hall, which had recently experienced a significant reduction in population density.

So I might have been the last man on earth as I wandered both floors of the new wing, the conservatory, and finally the grounds, where I spotted another living creature in the form of the yet to be named goat. He looked at me guardedly, as though I might have some claim on his lawn, and then, dismissing me with a cordial nod, he returned to his labours. It wasn't until I circumnavigated the new wing to the tradesman's entrance that I encountered a fellow two-legged guest of the castle, this time behaving even more furtively than the goat.

The kitchen door opened, seemingly on its own, and then the cloth cap of List Porter appeared. He looked this way and that, spotted me, and then disappeared. A moment later he stepped out the door and pulled it closed behind him.

"'Day, Mister Boisjoly," he said. "Lovely morning."

"Are you leaving us, Porter?"

He nodded. "And I'd be obliged if that were to remain between you and me, Mister Boisjoly. That inspector fellow can be quite demanding on a man's time, and the Hare's Foot wants opening."

"Opening time isn't for hours," I pointed out.

"True, sir," said Porter. "But there's the inn needs seeing to... two guests, on the same night mind. It's more than one man can handle."

"You should take on help, Porter," I suggested. "Now that flocks of London property developers have discovered our little corner of paradise you won't have a moment's peace."

"Sound advice," agreed Porter. "But Fray is a small village, as you know sir, and it has a likewise small pool of those who aspire to a career in the hospitality industry."

"London's a big town," I lamented right along with him, "and I couldn't trap a decent valet with a butterfly net."

"My deepest commiserations, Mister Boisjoly," said Porter. "Life must be very trying for you."

"It is, Porter. If it weren't for Carnaby, that's the steward at my club, I'd likely starve in the streets."

Porter nodded and rocked on his heels with his hands in

his pockets. There's a very specific way in which men, under certain conditions, will nod and rock on their heels with their hands in their pockets. The action typically comes at the end of an exchange of small talk, and is intended to convey something along the lines of 'Pleasantries having been exchanged, let us politely go our separate ways.'

"What can you tell me, Porter, about the major's will?" I asked, folding my arms over my chest, a widely accepted counter-manoeuvre to nodding and rocking on heels with hands in pockets.

"Nothing at all, sir," said Porter.

I held the line. My arms remained resolutely crossed, my sceptical gaze seeking Porter's evasive eye.

"I can tell you that it was written in 1889, prior to the major's commission to Africa," confessed Porter at last. "This was before Mister Fairfax and Mister Harold were born, you understand, and so it had the peculiar characteristic of naming benefactors what didn't yet exist — any and all Evelyn Canterfells."

"I see," I said. "So why not change the will once the family had produced a matching set of Evelyns?"

"Expense, primarily," said Porter. "The nearest solicitor to Fray is in Hastings, and so the legal party in question is a London firm with a very posh address in Threadneedle Street. In any case, I don't believe that the major was satisfied with just the two Evelyns, particularly since they developed minds of their own, and interests somewhat far afield of what the major might have described as those of gentlemen."

"Such as the military."

"Mainly that, yes sir."

"He was keeping open the prospect that more Evelyns might be added to the collection."

"That has long been my belief, yes sir."

"So the estate is to be divided evenly between everyone named Evelyn Canterfell?"

"Not entirely, no," said Porter, glancing longingly in the direction of the Hare's Foot. "There's consideration for Mister Halliwell and Mister Sebastian, God rest his soul, and bits and bobs for the estate and the village, and it's not just any Evelyn Canterfell who shares what remains, just the Evelyn Canterfells descended from the major."

"Doesn't that go without saying?"

"You would think so, yes sir, but when word of the nature of the will somehow became common knowledge there was a spate of villagers legally changing their names or christening their children Evelyn Canterfell Wheatley, Evelyn Canterfell Finchley, Evelyn Canterfell Spooner, and so on, including boys and girls and, to my certain knowledge, at least one donkey."

"How did that pan out?"

"I suppose it remains to be seen, but there's a reason them Threadneedle Street solicitors ask upwards of ninety-two pounds six to prepare and administer a will."

"To be clear, then, Porter, the only significant beneficiaries from the death of Major Canterfell are Fiddles and Hal."

"And Mister Halliwell who, as remaining son, receives a stipend."

"What about Mrs Canterfell?"

"As Mister Sebastian's widow, sir," said Porter, "she would get nothing, seeing as her husband predeceased his father."

"Nothing? At all?" I said.

"Not according to the will."

"But if Sebastian had died after the major, Mrs Canterfell

would have had his stipend for life," I said.

"Yes," confirmed Porter.

"Odd that the major doesn't appear to have considered Laetitia."

"Oh?" said Porter, loading the syllable high with meaning. "Why would that be odd, Mister Boisjoly?"

"Oh, just idle supposition," I claimed. "Well, thank you, Porter, this has been most illuminating."

"Glad to be of service, Mister Boisjoly," said Porter. "Now, if you'll forgive me, I must see to my duties at the inn."

"The inn has gambolled along quite nicely without you for four hundred years, Porter, and the tavern for even longer," I said. "And I have it on good authority — my own, if I may be so bold — that the inspector will be requiring your presence in the conservatory this afternoon."

"Me, Mister Boisjoly?" said Porter. "Surely I'm what the authorities call a 'bystander', as regards the affair."

"I suppose that depends, Porter, on to which affair it is that you refer."

Porter nodded shrewdly, as though to signal agreement on a delicate philosophical point. He continued to regard me this way until I was forced to put my hands in my pockets and rock on my heels. Porter acknowledged receipt of the message by doffing his cloth cap and then ducking back into the tradesman's entrance. From within I heard Luna yelp with surprise.

CHAPTER SIXTEEN
The Intriguing Identity of Powderkeg Malone

I continued my tour of the perimeter and found Mallet, clearing the drainage canals next to the driveway.

"Should you be missing him at any point, Mallet," I said on approach, "you'll find your goat on the other side of the house."

"I know that, Mister Boisjoly," said Mallet, glancing up from his hoe and then glancing back down. "That's why I'm on this side of the house."

"That serves my purposes well," I said. "It's best the goat doesn't hear what I have to say. Did you happen to hear a gunshot last night, around quarter to eight?"

"I did, sir. It was hard to miss. I understand the major has been vanquished by the only soldier who could."

"Indeed," I said. "Nicely put. Might I ask where you were at the time?"

"I was below-stairs, sir, sharing a digestive tipple with Miss Lively."

"That tallies, then," I said. "If she'll account for you then everyone has an alibi for when the gun went off."

"I can't say for a certainty that Miss Lively can account for my presence, sir," said Mallett, leaning forward to infer a zone of confidentiality. "She referred to me by several names as the evening progressed, not all of which was my own."

"That also tallies," I said. "So, unless the major shot himself, that leaves only a stranger, who would have to have leapt from the first-floor window."

"A stranger, sir?" asked Mallet, now satisfied with the little river he'd created between the gravel and lawn, he leaned on his hoe.

"It's the only other possibility. No one could have descended the tower in the time it took us to reach the stairs, and Lydde and I searched all the way to the roof."

"Begging your pardon, sir," said Mallet. "It's not the only other possibility."

"Really?" I said. "Continue, Mallett, your words intrigue me. What is the other possibility?"

"I've no heavenly idea, sir," said Mallet. "I only mean to say it's not possible for a stranger to have jumped from the tower."

"It seems unlikely, I know," I agreed, "but to quote Sherlock Holmes, once we have eliminated the impossible, whatever remains..."

"No offence to your friend Mister Holmes," said Mallet earnestly, "but even if someone could survive the fall, the turf was a swamp last night. He'd have sunk two foot deep and still be there this morning, or he'd have left some very deep tracks."

"No tracks?"

"No tracks, Mister Boisjoly."

"I see," I said, stroking my chin with the stoic resolve with which I imagine Holmes would have received reports of the disappointing comportment of the dog in the night.

"Well, I don't mind saying, you've let me down, Mallet," I said. "You can redeem yourself, though, by keeping Miss Lively sober long enough to attend to the inspector this afternoon in the conservatory, do you think you can manage that?"

"Keep Miss Lively from the bottle?" he asked. "No, sir, I don't believe I can."

"No, I don't suppose I could either, not with the help of three strong men," I conceded. "Very well, see if you can at least tempt her to the conservatory this afternoon, will you?"

"I'll see to it, sir."

I skipped back into the house, feeling like a man who gets things done. I expect the mood was much like that which must come over that Henry Ford chap when he pushes another jalopy off the end of his assembly line. In the main hall I met Vickers, looking like a man who'd entered a room and forgotten why.

"Vickers, just the man I wanted to see, among others," I said. "Do you know the location of the rest of the staff?"

The old eyes focused on me for a moment. "Mister…" he said, and I could almost see the pages flipping back through time, epoch o'erleaping epoch, all the way to breakfast, "…Boisjoly. I believe that Mister Lydde, Miss Malone, and Miss Lively are below-stairs."

"Stick to them like glue, Vickers," I said. "The inspector will be requiring their presence in the conservatory this afternoon, tea-ish. Stick to yourself like glue as well, you will also be required."

"Very good, sir."

Vickers stood his ground and wavered, as though in a light breeze.

"Were you on your way, somewhere, Vickers?"

"Below-stairs, sir."

"I see. Carry on."

Vickers looked left and then right. Then he turned in a circle on the spot.

"Through the drawing-room," I said, indicating the hall to the left of the tower stairs, "past the dining room, first door on the right."

"I'm very much obliged, sir," said Vickers, and shuffled off.

I followed as far as the tower stairs, and then took a hard right to the glassed terrace, which to my mind had become the natural habitat of the common and garden Harold. My instincts had failed me, however, and though any time in the past I'd seen the terrace or even heard it spoken of it was positively teeming with Harolds, now there was only his wicker chair, bearing lonely testament. I decided to give my instincts a chance to restore themselves and, like the stealthy spider who reposes in his web and lets his prey do all the leg work, I fitted myself into the chair.

Moments later the strategy bore fruit, and Hal wandered in after me.

"There you are," he said. "I've been looking all over for you."

"That was wise," I said. "I've been all over. I was looking for you, too, as it happens."

"Never mind that, Anty," said Hal, dropping into a matching wicker armchair, "you never told us how it was done."

"I can say with some certainty that your grandfather was not shot by an intruder who then leapt from the first-floor window, relying on the earth, softened by heavy rains, to break his fall."

"That's rather specific. How do you know that's not what happened?"

"Tracks, my dear boy," I said. "There would be tracks, there, before us in the lawn."

Hal looked out at the garden. "Yes, I suppose there would be. I hadn't thought of that."

"Some of us just have the gift."

He sat in silence, meditating, presumably, on the lawn and its vexing absence of deep tracks.

"Anty?" he said, finally, looking at me. "Don't you think something rather odd is going on here at Canterfell Hall?"

"You know, Hal, I do," I said.

"I don't just mean the tracks, you understand."

"No," I agreed. "That does seem to fall more into the category of symptom."

"I was referring to two mysterious deaths, a peerage in abeyance, some very strange behaviour by my mother with regards Grandpapa..."

"And let's not leave out that goat," I added. "A very shifty character if ever I've seen one."

Hal glanced out again at the lawn and, sure enough, at that very moment the goat was fouling the fountain canal and simultaneously holding our gaze like a boxer stepping into the ring.

"You were beholding this very panorama at your father's departure time, if memory serves," I said.

"Mmm," mmm'd Hal, in the affirmative tone.

"What else did you see, Hal?"

"What else?"

"Yes. Did you see the goat, for instance?"

"No," he said. "Anyway, I thought you said that the goat had left?"

"He did," I confirmed. "The gardener has since repatriated the beast, exercising admirable willpower, I might add."

"Yes, that's right," said Hal. "I saw the gardener. He was there, by the lake."

"I see."

"Does that tell you something useful, Anty?" asked Hal, his voice ringing with boyish hope.

"I'm afraid so," I said. "That's exactly where the gardener said he was."

"So you've got it all sorted out?"

"Short of a couple of details," I said, "I've had a few setbacks in the past minute or so."

"I mean, it's why Fairfax asked you down, isn't it?" said Hal. "I always admired that about you."

"My unnatural knack for cracking the tough nut, you mean?"

"No," said Hal. "Well, yes, that too, obviously, but I mean your loyalty to your friends."

"Your cousin was my coxswain," I said with the resolution of a second-tier Oxford rowing man. "You don't forget a thing like that."

"Lucky for Fairfax."

"I regard all my friends as equally fortunate," I said, distracted by a new line of enquiry. "Can you do me a small service, Hal, and hasten to the conservatory this afternoon? I ask on behalf of the inspector."

"Do you think he's figured out who killed my father and the major?"

"Oh, good heavens, no," I said. "Probably wants to search the house again, or have an audience while he beats a confession out of the downstairs staff with a rubber hose. Talking of which, do you know where one would find your mother at this hour?"

"In her room, I believe," said Hal. "I heard Luna say that she was bringing her a tray."

"Capital," I said, leaping to my feet. "See you in the conservatory, say, tea time."

Laetitia's room, I reasoned, would be the one she once shared with her husband, as opposed to the Chartreuse Room which, speaking euphemistically, she didn't. I tapped on the door and, sure enough, I was greeted with an amiable "Go away."

"It's me, Mrs Canterfell," I said, "Anty Boisjoly. I wondered if you'd like someone to talk to about what happened yesterday."

There was a pause, explained an instant later by the melancholy tones of ice clattering about the bottom of an empty lowball.

"Come in," said Laetitia, with the resigned sigh of the habitué, ordering a last pint just under the bell.

"Good day, Mister Boisjoly." Laetitia was occupying two chairs before the floor-to-ceiling French doors — she reclined in one embroidered Louis XIV and her feet were on another. She was wearing a dressing gown that appeared to be composed of many different layers or, perhaps, many different dressing gowns, and she looked like an unmade bed. The room was of a baroque aesthetic and everything reflected light, even the wallpaper, and it occurred to me that this room would be an appalling place to wake up on the morning of a hard night. "Would you care for some tea?"

"Thank you."

"There isn't any tea," she said, gesturing with her glass toward the tray. "Have a drink."

"All the better," I said, helping myself to the ice bucket and decanter from the tray to which Hal had doubtless earlier alluded. I swirled them together in the glass, rendering the happy clattering music that I find brings cheer to almost any atmosphere. I held up the decanter and Laetitia held up her glass, a silent agreement was reached, and I loosed a generous portion onto her lonesome ice.

"May I?" I gestured to a meagre footstool at the end of the bed, and Laetitia acquiesced with a grimace that expressed clearly that I could sit on top of the wardrobe for all she cared.

"You saw the major yesterday," I said.

"I don't even know you, Boisjoly," she said, addressing me, presumably, but looking out the window. "And you're the only person who knows my most intimate secret."

"When I was a boy growing up in Kensington, our house was one of three which shared a coal cellar," I said. "One day, someone with access to that cellar wrote something quite seditious about our next-door neighbour but one, Elliot Lord Doncaster, Twelfth Baron of Hittlesham, on the garden walls of all three houses with a piece of coal."

"Thank you," said Laetitia, "that is a most distracting tale."

"It's not finished yet," I said, holding up a 'bear with me' hand. "My father, not without reason, assumed that it was I who had defaced the garden wall, but I knew that the real subversive was the Right Honourable Elliot Junior, owing to the boy's unique spelling of the word 'distended'. I presented him with the facts and, seizing the moment, he swore me to secrecy, an oath I have kept to this day, in spite of going without pocket money for a month, and being made to remove the offending remarks myself, with a wire boot brush."

"I see," said Laetitia. "And why are you telling me this?"

"I feel at liberty to do so, now," I explained. "Elliot the younger told the story as the ice breaker at his wedding last year."

"I mean, why are you telling me about it at all?"

"As evidence of my proud history of unyielding discretion," I explained. "Your affair with your father-in-law is for you and you alone to divulge, should you ever choose to do so."

"I'm not referring to my affair with the major, Boisjoly. I'm referring to the fact that I killed him."

"You didn't kill him," I said.

"Maybe not directly, but I put him into the state of mind to do it himself."

"What did you say to him?"

Laetitia looked into her drink.

"I reminisced," she said.

"Ah."

"Yes, ah," she agreed. "He remembered feelings and details, but the history was gone."

"Details?" I asked. "What sort of details?"

"The painting, for example," she said, swirling her ice, as one does, for inspiration. "I told him that it was I who hid it, because the inspector was looking for his damned codicil."

"What did he remember of that?"

"The poem. You were right, by the way, the word was 'Begum'."

"I'm very gratified." I inclined my head modestly. "Anything else?"

Laetitia shook her head and blinked something out of her eyes.

"Just details," she said. "He recalled the name of the hotel in Paris where we spent the week he was back from the Boer War, but he didn't remember the Boer War."

"Well, what of it?" I said, rising from the footstool for dramatic effect and because I was losing feeling in my lower legs. "Wars come and go. It seems to me perfidious Albion is always either finishing, fighting, or fomenting conflict somewhere in the world. The major didn't forget the Boer War, he probably just lost count, but a true love affair, with Paris junkets to discreet hotels with unobstructed views of the Eiffel Tower... did this hotel have unobstructed views of the Eiffel Tower, Mrs Canterfell?"

"Breathtaking. With a balcony."

"...a true love affair with discreet hotels and unobstructed views of the Eiffel Tower, that's something worth remembering. I hope that when I reach the major's advanced years that I, too, forget all discord, to make room among my souvenirs for the abundance of romance."

"Admirable effort, Boisjoly," said Laetitia. She'd been watching my performance but now returned her unappreciative gaze to the shining summer's day. "The man was broken. The last thing he said to me was that he needed to put an end to all this nonsense."

"That's what he said? It's time to put an end to all this nonsense?"

She nodded.

"Did he happen to specify to which nonsense he referred?" I asked. "The major always struck me as someone who had a low tolerance for all manner of nonsense."

Laetitia trained a weary eye on me but said nothing.

"More tea?" I said, holding up the decanter.

Laetitia held up her glass and I obliged.

"I expect you hear this rather a lot, Boisjoly," she said.

"What's that?"

"I wish to be alone."

"Right ho, Mrs Canterfell," I said, replacing the decanter and withdrawing to safety. "Incidentally, I don't believe for a moment that you think the major killed himself. Perhaps you'll join us in the conservatory around tea time, while I explain why to the inspector."

I pattered up the hall and tapped on the door of the Rose Room, eliciting a tinkly "Who is it?" from within.

"It's me, Miss Pierpoint," I said. "Anty Boisjoly."

There was a slight pause as, I gathered, Rosalind approached the door before whispering, "Are you only Mister Boisjoly?"

"Do you mean, am I alone?" I whispered back. "Because yes, I am."

The door opened wide enough for Rosalind's shapely head to slip through, peer both ways, smile an embarrassed sort of smile, and then withdraw, pulling me along in its wake.

"Are you preparing to leave us?" I asked, closing the door discreetly behind me, as seemed appropriate to the furtive mood of the room. Rosalind was dressed very gamely in a tweed motoring outfit, including trousers and a linen waistcoat, in the androgynous fashion which was coming at us at the time from France. Her hair was packed tightly and so were her bags, except for a chaos of camera gear, which apparently she'd been strapping into canvas tubes and wooden boxes when I knocked on the door.

"I think it's for the best," said Rosalind, busying herself with a carton of flashbulbs, like two dozen eggs open on the bed.

"But what about Fiddles?" I asked. "He's potty for you. It'll break his heart."

"Isn't he going to be arrested for murder?"

"You know about that, do you?" I said. "Well, you could wait for him."

"I understand that he's likely to hang."

"So you won't have to wait very long."

"I really think that I need to go, Mister Boisjoly." Rosalind held a bulb to her ear and then, having passed judgement, dropped it into a wicker basket next to the writing desk. "People keep dying at Canterfell Hall."

"That does seem to be the latest craze, doesn't it?" I conceded. "It'll probably pass."

"Will you tell Fairfax that I'm sorry, and that I hope they don't hang him?"

"Of course, Miss Pierpoint."

"Please," she said. "Call me Rosalind."

"With pleasure," I said. "And you must call me Powderkeg Malone."

She smiled at me vacantly. "But, your name isn't Powderkeg Malone, is it?"

"To my lasting regret, it is not," I confirmed. "But then, your name's not Rosalind Pierpoint, is it?"

CHAPTER SEVENTEEN
The Obscure Origins of *Quite Right, Milord*

As I rove back to my room I was aware of a serene sense of order, like the major must have often felt just before charging the flanks or flanking the charge, or whatever, and casting a fatherly eye over his rank of zealous Punjabis, all in bright red coats and shiny brass buttons and forming a perfect line. I recall gaining a similar sense of satisfaction prior to setting in motion the delicately aligned series of players and ploys that came to be known, in Boisjoly family lore, as the Mad Hatter's Tea Party.

As I recall it, I'd come down from Eton for the weekend, so I would have been no more than fifteen and at the early ascendency of my talent for unsticking the sticky situation. My father must have confused the dates and forgotten that Mama was due home that same weekend from her annual tune-up in the healing waters of Monte Carlo, because he was three sheets to the wind and about to unfurl the mizzen when I arrived. Had she seen him in this condition, again, we'd all have been in for a sub-zero weekend of walking on frozen eggshells, so something had to be done.

It was too late to sober the old man up, so in a fit of inspiration of the order which drove Archimedes from his bath, I hastily arranged a game of Quite Right, Milord, and invited as many neighbours as were on hand on a Saturday afternoon. The rules of Quite Right, Milord are simple, but gameplay can be quite complex; one person starts by saying something absurd, and the next person in order, typically sitting to the predecessor's left, responds to it with a comment which is somehow both pertinent and yet even more absurd. Should a player fail to respond in time, or answer with something sensible, the other participants all shout 'Quite Right, Milord', and the player is eliminated from that round. The winner is the last player remaining. I had to carefully explain the rules to all the guests because, until that day, Quite Right, Milord didn't exist.

It was the moment before my mother walked through the door, tired and touchy and predisposed to quick judgement, that I had that same sentiment of all ducks present, accounted for, and aligned. Elliot Lord Doncaster was there, always game for a new wheeze, as was Sir Cedric Strange, the magistrate who lived in the house facing us across the square, the sisters Hathaway who lived next door to him, several strangers that I'd conscripted from a picnic in the park, and the Venerable Jocelyn Jones, Archdeacon of Kensington. Everyone had a cup of tea and was primed and keen to play a rollicking round of Quite Right, Milord, except my father who, in his current state, didn't need to be told to say something absurd.

And it went off without a hitch. Mama stepped into the parlour just as my father gave forth upon a proposal that pigeons should be made to pay taxes — a favourite theme of his when in his cups. My mother was about to make the familiar accusation when Sir Cedric seconded the motion, and added that they should further be compelled to wear hats, so that we can tell the boy pigeons from the girls. Lord Doncaster dismissed this as unenforceable, but took the view that once pigeons had been subsumed into the system of taxation, they would obviously take to wearing hats voluntarily.

My mother listened to this market of ideas for a couple of rounds, and then made her excuses and went upstairs to lie down. The game continued until sundown and the Venerable Jones proved so adept that it was generally assumed that he was an old hand, brought in as a dark horse. It was as everyone was saying good night that I recalled that he had arrived too late to be briefed on the rules of Quite Right, Milord, and was in fact as tight as an owl.

I mused on this and other past glories for a measure of time lost to the impenetrable mists of the afternoon kip and was summoned back to consciousness by the chirping of, I'm going to say, a woodlark, in the absence of any ornithological expertise at all, in time for tea. The Blue Room, like all the guest rooms, enjoys two high windows, and the warmth and light of a sympathetic sun on summer afternoons. The sashes were raised on said windows and the curtains undulated on gentle breezes. Leaf, lawn, and lake shimmered English green and limpid blue and collected, collated, and conveyed the visceral scents of the countryside into my room. I allowed myself a moment's pause to drink it all in, before bringing this pleasant scene crashing down around our ears.

Then I wandered down to the conservatory. As I approached, from beyond the closed door, I heard the boisterous babble of a household in gentle discord. I distinctly heard a genial "Oh, do be quiet, Mother," a playful "You blithering old man," and the amiable smashing of a china cup.

"What ho, Canterfells," I said, making my entrance. Nine sets of glowering eyes beneath nine deeply furrowed brows turned on me at once.

"What's the meaning of this, Boisjoly?" demanded Laetitia.

"Teatime?" I said. "Tradition, mainly. One of the countless verses of the song of our sceptred isle. Are those petit-fours?"

"You said that the inspector wanted us gathered in the conservatory," insisted Hal.

This claim was repeated, in their own words and simultaneously, by Luna, Lydde, Miss Lively, Mallet, and Porter. Fiddles and Vickers, who were otherwise engaged in a conspiracy against a teapot, demurred.

"Did I say that?" I asked. "I was speculating out loud, I think, that Inspector Wittersham would certainly want us all to be present when the murderer of Sebastian Canterfell and the major was revealed."

This was received by the assemblage in much the way a rowdy saloon at the apogee of a drunken brawl receives a sixgun fired in the air by an itinerant gunslinger with a dodgy past but a heart of gold. The murmuring ceased, and the eyebrows took flight.

"Are you saying that Wittersham knows the identity of the killer?" asked Fiddles.

"I suppose he might, but I very much doubt it," I said. "Does anyone know where he is, incidentally?"

And as though they'd been standing off-stage waiting for

their cue, Ivor and Hug came into the conservatory.

"Mister Canterfell?" said Ivor.

"Yes?" said Fiddles and Hal in harmony.

"Mister Evelyn — Fairfax — Canterfell," clarified Ivor.

"Yes, Inspector?" said Fiddles.

"I'm arresting you, sir, for the murder of Sebastian Canterfell."

"Again?" I asked. "You really must resist the power this habit of arresting Fiddles for murder has over you, Inspector. Once or twice, of course, one can easily see the allure, but like everything which can prove habit-forming, it must be taken in its measure."

"Please be quiet, Mister Boisjoly," said Ivor. "Constable, arrest this man."

"What, ostensibly, has changed?" I asked. "Word on the street has it that you have insufficient cause to hold Fiddles for the murder of Sebastian Canterfell."

"Only this," said Ivor, withdrawing a chip of stone from his pocket.

"What is it?" I asked. "Some sort of note?"

"It is an arrowhead," said Ivor, somewhat irascibly. "One of those which of late was housed in the pyramid box stolen from the gallery. It was found on the floor in Mister Canterfell's room."

"Surely this is more of a housekeeping issue than a matter of prosecutorial procedure," I observed. "Well, Luna, what have you got to say for yourself?"

"Oh, there it is," said Lydde. "It always comes down to the proletariat."

Luna, in her defence, buried her head in her hands and sobbed.

Miss Lively placed a maternal hand on the maid's slight

and shivering shoulder and softly whispered, "Quit your blubbering."

"Mister Canterfell, do you deny breaking into the gallery and stealing the major's pyramid chest?" asked Ivor, once again understudying the barrister he probably would have been had he only applied himself in Latin class.

"Categorically," said Fiddles, as someone who actually did apply himself in Latin class. "And even if I had taken the chest, an absurd contention on its face, what would that establish?"

"It's a breach of your bail conditions," said Ivor. "Destroying evidence, and interfering with the police in the discharge of their duties."

"Preposterous," said Fiddles. "What evidence?"

"I should have thought that would be obvious," said Ivor, "the Canterfell codicil."

"Obviously you searched my room," said Fiddles. "Did you find the codicil?"

"You destroyed it," said Ivor. "Doubtless it amended the major's will to your disadvantage. The major's untimely death accelerated your plans, and you were left with no choice but to risk exposure by breaking into the gallery, retrieving and, ultimately, destroying the codicil."

"Is this true, Fairfax?" said Hal.

"Of course it's not true, Hal," said Fiddles. "The inspector is of the single-minded stripe of plodder who, once he's fixed on a suspect, won't hear anything to the contrary, preferring instead to fit the evidence to the theory."

"On the contrary, Mister Canterfell," said Ivor. "The facts prove indisputably that you were the only person who could have been in the gallery when the bees..."

"Hoverflies," I interjected.

"Thank you… when the hoverflies were introduced into your uncle's study," said Ivor. "That fact alone will hang you."

Fiddles fixed me with the look trapeze artists give other trapeze artists who, at the critical moment, have to'd when they were meant to have fro'd.

"Well, Fiddles?" I said. "Did you kill your uncle? We can't entirely discount the possibility."

"Of course not," he said.

"Well, somebody did," I said. "What's more, somebody murdered the major, too, Inspector, and the killer is in this room at this very moment."

CHAPTER EIGHTEEN
The Momentous Meaning of the Major's Mistaken Memories

"The major most certainly was not murdered," said Ivor. "The door to the gallery was locked from the inside, the major was shot, once, through the head, and he held in his hand his sidearm, from which a single bullet had been discharged."

"Surely that all points to foul play," I said.

Ivor folded his arms and looked at me beneath hooded eyes.

"Very well, Mister Boisjoly," he said. "Please explain how a room locked from the inside, a shot to the head, and the weapon in the hand of the deceased, suggests to you anything other than suicide."

"Quite sure, Inspector?" I asked. "You wouldn't prefer to just summarily execute Fiddles?"

"Quite sure, Mister Boisjoly."

"Very well," I said. "You say that a single shot was fired from the gun. How do you know this?"

"Apart from the fact that we all heard the shot," said Ivor. "The weapon in question is the major's service revolver. The chamber contains up to six shots, five were remaining, and the weapon had recently been discharged."

"And that doesn't strike you as suspicious," I said, with a tone that resonated worryingly of Mister Speakes, my last Latin master at Eton, whose chief characteristic as a teacher was an enduring faith in the instructive power of sarcasm.

"Should it?" asked Ivor.

"The major's sidearm has not seen service for twenty years," I said. "It hasn't been loaded since the Boer War. And now the major, planning to kill himself, fully loaded his revolver with six bullets? Are you proposing that he thought he might miss?"

"Doubtless it was by force of habit," said Ivor, without conviction. "The major was very set in his ways, I understand."

"So, you'll accept, on the testimony of his family, that the major was of a dogmatic nature, but not that he would be boiled in vinegar before he'd take his own life," I said.

"I have to agree, Inspector," added Hal. "Grandpapa was extremely duty-bound. I think he considered despair a moral failing somewhere between cowardice and disrespecting the uniform."

"And as for the door, Inspector," I continued. "What makes you say that it had been locked from the inside? Both you and Hug were able to peer through the keyhole."

"Constable Pennybun almost certainly knocked the key from the door when he tried to open it," said Ivor. "It was on the floor, next to the door."

"The major never locks the door to the gallery, though," I said. "He doesn't even carry a key."

"I think it's fair to say that the major has never killed himself before, either," said Ivor, with the reserve of a man trying not to laugh at his own joke. "But yesterday his son was murdered, and then someone drew from him the distressing revelation that he was losing his faculties."

"Setting that aside," I said, sharing a conspiratorial glance with Laetitia. "Let us consider the blood on the floor of the gallery. Can we draw any conclusions from that?"

"No," said Ivor. "We cannot. It was mostly diluted with rain, giving us very little in the way of guidance with regards to the disposition of the major."

"Exactly, Inspector," I said. "It is precisely this to which I would draw your attention."

Ivor glared at me with an intensity that required his eyebrows to join forces.

"The window was open," he said at last.

"The window was open," I confirmed. "It was a beautiful day, all day, until the storm swept abruptly upon us as they so often do this close to the sea, and yet the window was open."

"That doesn't change the time of death, though," said Ivor.

"No?" I said. "Then let us review another peculiarity of life at Canterfell Hall — the post."

"What's unusual about the post?"

"Nothing," I said. "On the contrary, it's notoriously reliable. So reliable, in fact, that a letter can be sent, as Fiddles so ably demonstrated, from someone at Canterfell Hall to someone else at Canterfell Hall, via the post office. And I can say with more than the average degree of expertise that it cannot be intercepted, once that letter is set upon its way."

"Are we still talking about the major?" asked Ivor.

"Most expressly yes, Inspector, we are," I assured him. "Even as we review the very precise mathematics of who was where when Sebastian Canterfell was driven from his study by what he thought were bees."

"Just so," said Ivor. "The arrangement of alibis that will hang Fairfax Canterfell."

"I very much hope that you'll get an opportunity to hang someone, Inspector, because it clearly plays heavily on your mind," I said. "But before you do, reminisce with me about those few fateful moments. Vickers hears a commotion in the study, and is unable to enter."

"Because the door had been glued shut by the killer," elucidated Ivor. "The commotion was Sebastian Canterfell trying to get out."

"Yes, and then Vickers seeks help in the conservatory, where he finds Fiddles."

"The court will be shown that Mister Fairfax positioned himself in the conservatory, knowing that Mister Vickers, being unfamiliar with the layout of Canterfell Hall, would go there," said Ivor.

"Let us stick to what we know, Inspector," I said. "Vickers saw Fiddles, and Mallet, you saw Vickers, is that correct?"

"Correct, sir," said Mallet, who had been gaping open-mouthed at the spectacle, and seemed pleased to finally have a line.

"And at the same time, and the moment when Mister Sebastian had his unfortunate disagreement with gravity, you saw Mister Harold, sitting in the terrace sunroom, correct?"

"That's right too," said Mallet, with an awed tone, as though I'd just produced a living rabbit from a tobacco pouch.

"Then Hal, you in turn saw Rosalind, who was in the drawing-room."

"Yes," said Hal.

"Confirmed by Lydde," I said, in the general direction of the butler.

"That's right," said Lydde, guardedly, like a man being invited to play Three Card Monte on Petticoat Lane.

"Meanwhile, the major and Mrs Canterfell alibi each other, as do Luna and Miss Lively."

"I was in the kitchen," said Miss Lively, with considerable conviction.

"Of course you were not in the kitchen, Miss Lively," I said. "But we'll take it as read that you cannot recall where you were. And finally, List Porter and the honourable Halliwell Canterfell account for each other's presence at the Hare's Foot inn."

Both men, as though choreographed, looked at each other and then at me and then nodded.

"Establishing, once again, Mister Boisjoly," said Ivor, "that Fairfax Canterfell is the only one with the means and opportunity to commit the murder."

"This would be so, Inspector," I said, "if everyone was telling the truth, including the accused."

"Which they are," said Ivor. "Each person's story is confirmed by someone else. No one of them can be lying."

"Exactly, Inspector. Not one of them is lying — two of them are."

"Who?" said Ivor. "And why?"

"Not why, Inspector, but how," I said. "Answering why gets us nowhere, because almost everyone in this room benefited from the death of Sebastian Canterfell. We know, for instance, that Miss Lively held a grudge against him for ruining what was objectively her only chance at love."

"*Mon cher Jules,*" moaned Miss Lively, with the clunky finesse of the drunken Englishwoman trying to speak French and producing something like the sound of an inexperienced journeyman stacking bricks.

"Lydde, too, resented the treatment of the previous staff at Sebastian Canterfell's hand, is that not so, Lydde?"

"I had no reason to kill anyone," said Lydde, defiantly. "The demise of the parasite class is an historical inevitability, hastened and assured by its own excesses."

"Indeed," I said. "Speaking of excesses, Porter, you openly admitted that you would benefit from the death of Sebastian Canterfell, if it would end his plans to allow development of Canterfell Wood."

"I was nowhere near Canterfell Hall when Mister Sebastian was killed," said Porter.

"Weren't you?" I asked. "The inn had only one guest at the time, and one alibi, Halliwell Canterfell..." At the mention of his name, the honourable member looked up from a plate stacked high with miniature pastries. "...who also objected to his brother's plans to develop the forest, in a plan which had the potential to radically change the voting demographic of Fray."

"I would also draw the attention of the house to the impact this proposed development would have had on the natural habitat of the badger," added Halliwell, before returning his attention to his plate of petit-fours.

"And Mrs Canterfell," I continued, "you knew that if your husband predeceased you that you would inherit his stipend, and right to reside at Canterfell Hall indefinitely."

"Other way round, Mister Boisjoly," said Porter. "Mrs Canterfell gets nothing in the will."

"Not the will, Porter," I said. "The codicil. Mrs Canterfell pretended to not know the contents of the codicil, and took the position that she could never know, because the major had forgotten that he'd written it. Believing this, though, requires us to also believe that the major lost his memory thirty years ago, when he had cause to make confidential arrangements for the disposal of his estate. Of course the document accommodates for Mrs Canterfell, and of course she knew it."

"How dare you, Boisjoly," said Laetitia.

"Is this true, mother?" asked Hal.

"Please, Hal," I said. "Do you expect me to believe that your mother didn't tell you all? You know what's in the codicil, and you know why, and that's why you, too, had cause to murder your father."

"It never ends," lamented Hal. "You've persecuted me since we were at school."

"Evidently not enough," I said. "Perhaps if we'd taken a firmer line with respect to sconcing and pennying in your junior year we might have succeeded in breaking the apron strings."

"Steady on, old man," said Fiddles.

"And Fiddles, of course, remains the crowd favourite," I said, "as the methodical departures of his uncle and grandfather, in that specific order, puts him in line to inherit the earldom of Fray, clearing an easy path to government office without the bother of contesting an election."

"But I had no way of knowing that," said Fiddles.

"Of course you did, Fiddles," I scoffed. "You knew that your grandfather had very little time remaining and that your father would never abide by the peculiar conditions of the writ. Even Hal knew that, which is the whole point, isn't it Hal?"

"What do you mean?" said Hal into his teacup.

"Don't you wonder, Inspector, why it is that we haven't seen the codicil yet?" I asked.

"Because it's been destroyed, obviously," said Ivor.

"It most certainly has not," I said. "It's far too valuable. You see the codicil was written to address the major's two secret fears — that Mrs Canterfell would be neglected after he passed, and that his name would be forgotten. He addressed the issue of his legacy in his will — the bulk of his estate is divided among any benefactors who have his name."

"The two Evelyns," said Ivor.

"There are dozens," I said. "Aren't there Porter?"

"Several, sir, yes," said Porter.

"The major didn't want to discourage the practice of persisting his name, but he didn't want his fortune going to any donkeys named Evelyn. So he added a secret article in the codicil. What does it say, Hal?" I asked.

"I don't know what you mean."

"Perhaps you could just hand it over, then, and we can read it aloud," I said.

"What makes you think he's got it?" asked Ivor.

"The early morning post," I said. "The killer was too clever by half, and the manner of dispatching Sebastian Canterfell left a scene that we all took to be evidence of a frenzied search. Consequently, Inspector, you announced a further and exhaustive search of the castle and, with no time to properly hide the codicil, Hal simply addressed it to himself, and put it in plain view in the outgoing mail tray in the hall. To be certain that it was out of sight by the time your efforts began in the morning, he invented a pretext to send Lydde to the post office before you arrived."

"The telegram," said Lydde.

"Exactly," I said. "The telegram to Halliwell Canterfell, in Westminster. After the inspector described his encounter with an eccentric preoccupied with Edmond Ironsides, Fiddles, I, and above all, Hal, would have known that the honourable member was at the Hare's Foot Tavern, not half an hour away, and yet Hal sent him a telegram in London. When the mail came back the next day there were two letters, the misguided note that Fiddles had accidentally sent to Rosalind, and one for Hal — the codicil."

Hal peeked up from his teacup. "It was just for safe-keeping," he said.

"I've no doubt," I said. "So perhaps you'll hand it over now."

"I think it should wait until the reading of the will," said Hal. "They're sort of a matching pair."

"And that's the real objective, isn't it Hal?" I said. "You've had the codicil since your father, following tradition, handed it over to you and you, ignoring tradition, opened it and read it. And what you read there told you that it must remain secret until after the demise of the major."

"I was only protecting my mother's good name," said Hal, and then he reached into his breast pocket and withdrew a long, thin, yellowing envelope.

"Is that..." began Fiddles.

"It is," I said, and took the envelope from Hal.

CHAPTER NINETEEN
The Contents of the Canterfell Codicil

The envelope had long ago been secured by a wax seal stamped, it appeared, with a service medal. The wax had recently been surgically separated from the paper and resealed, I would have guessed, with carpet glue. I opened the envelope and withdrew a single sheet of heavy paper, folded in three. It was written in elegant long-form and signed, at the bottom, Evelyn Clarence Canterfell, Captain, 19th Royal Hussars, June 1st, 1898, and it was witnessed by a Captain Avery Mannering-Jones, the same date, at Fort William, Bengal Presidency.

The introduction was formal and acknowledged the existence of a will lodged with a Threadneedle Street solicitor, and then said some uncomfortably kind things about Laetitia Canterfell that caused me to glance at her and see her in a younger, happier light.

"This, I think, is the key article," I said, and then read, "...the remains of the estate shall be divided evenly among directly descending boys named Evelyn Canterfell, and only Evelyn Canterfell, and only on the condition that the beneficiary's name has not been changed, amended or appended by English law."

"Seems reasonable," said Ivor. "If people were changing their names to Evelyn Canterfell in an effort to get a share."

"If that's how it's interpreted, it is reasonable," I said. "But in his zeal to protect the purity of the line, the major has overstepped it. What do you make of it from a legal perspective, Fiddles?"

Fiddles was staring daggers at his cousin. "It means that I, as Lord Bunce, Fourth Earl of Fray, inherit nothing."

"Which brings us finally to why, Inspector," I said. "Money is why. Specifically the entire, vast, Canterfell estate, including ten thousand shares of the Bengal Savings and Loan, and a stable in Berkshire, with two winners last year at Epsom. You were right about this much — Sebastian Canterfell was murdered to divert the earldom to the cadet line, but not because Fiddles wanted to be Lord Bunce, rather because Hal did not."

"I thought you said the key was how," said Ivor. "Harold Canterfell was seen at the time of the murder in the terrace sunroom by the gardener."

"Hal's role in the disposal of his father was to provide an alibi to the real killer," I said, "the woman calling herself Rosalind Pierpoint."

"What?" said Fiddles. "Rosalind? I know I've said this before, Anty, and usually only in jest, but you're potty as a jam shop. Rosalind? A murderer?"

"Her name is not Rosalind," I said. "And she's not a distant cousin, twice removed, to Laetitia. A suspicion I've had since she claimed that she'd been contacted by a solicitor in Fray."

"Fray has no solicitor," said Hug.

"Hence my suspicions," I said. "Further confirmed when I was improvising a message to her from Fiddles, into which I poured all that I knew about her home state of Maine. In spite of ostensibly being among the pillars of the Maine Pierpoints, however, Rosalind didn't notice that I was talking absolute rot."

"She was polite enough to not correct your mistakes, and that makes her a murderer?" scoffed Fiddles.

"Your mistakes," I said. "At least, that's what she thought and, if you believe her story, which I do, she was quite off you at the time. I read your letter, the real letter, I mean, and from it I gathered that the source of the dispute was your curiosity about her family and friends."

"Yes, I suppose it was," said Fiddles. "So?"

"Rosalind's story was that she was a distant relative, profiting from the famous hospitality the English privileged class shows its own," I said. "This artifice was adequate cover for an imposter in a manor house — history tells us that a medieval swindler enjoyed the largess of Canterfell Hall for several months while claiming to be Saxon King Harold II, fresh from a near thing at the Battle of Hastings — but it was frail defence indeed against the attentions of a besotted Fiddles. She had to put you off, so she called you a, what was it? Snouty Sue?"

"Nosey Parker," said Fiddles, meditatively.

"Quite sure?" I said. "Snouty Sue sounds more American."

"Quite sure."

"Nosey Parker it is, then," I conceded. "Either way, this freed her to continue the plan that she was executing on behalf of and in conspiracy with Hal. It was Rosalind who released the hoverflies into the study by way of the speaking tube in the gallery. That done, she hastened to the drawing-room. Hal never went to the drawing-room, as he claimed, but he didn't need to, because he and Rosalind had already agreed their stories. She just needed to be there before Lydde began his rounds."

"Where is Rosalind, anyway?" said Fiddles.

"That's not the question, Fiddles, trust me," I said. "The real question is, where was Rosalind when the major was killed?"

"She was in the drawing-room, with the rest of us," said Ivor.

"No, she was not," I said. "Let us return, now, to the theme of the open window, and couple it with three other phenomena... the pigeons shot off the roof of the Hare's Foot Inn, the door of the Saint George church, and the theft of the major's pyramid box."

"What possible relevance can there be to the church door?" asked Ivor.

"None," I said. "What is interesting is the absence of a door. When Rosalind returned from, according to her story, photographing the church, she was soaked to the bone. If she'd been caught in the rain, as she claimed, why didn't she just go into the church?"

"Fine," said Ivor. "We'll leave that one, weak as it is, what's this about pigeons?"

"Porter, when did you start noticing that the London property developers were shooting pigeons off your roof?" I asked.

"Coming on three weeks now."

"Roughly as long as Rosalind has been on the premises," I observed. "And finally, the theft of the pyramid box, Inspector, was no theft at all. It was cover, made necessary by your decision to lock the door to the gallery."

"Cover for what?" asked Ivor. "Was something else taken?"

"No," I said. "Something was returned. Did you know that the major once killed a man who was being eaten by a tiger?"

"Should I have?"

"I daresay yes, Inspector, you should, because if you had you might have noticed a rifle — the very long-range rifle that the major used to put a comrade out of his misery — was missing before the robbery, and no longer missing afterward."

"A long range rifle?" said Ivor, realisation waving over him.

"Very long range," I said. "Long enough to accurately shoot a man being consumed by a tiger from a safe distance, and certainly enough to hit pigeons on the roof of the Hare's Foot Inn from the relatively close range of the gallery window, as practice for making the same shot in the other direction."

The pause which followed this revelation allowed me to scan the faces in the room, which was a study in stunned still-life. The exception was Hal, who was squinting in a manner that I always took for vacant when at school, but now realised was something much more sinister.

"Hal set the scene," I said, looking at him but failing to catch his eye. "He loaded the service revolver and, probably earlier in the day, took it to the woods and fired a single shot. The noise would have been unnoticed... just another hunter interfering with the local wildlife. Then he returned the weapon to the gallery, placing it on the window sill, and said or did something which caused the major to go and see to it. Hal left him there, probably quietly locking the door from the outside, and then hastened to make himself an alibi, just in case. Then Rosalind, positioned at the treeline, no doubt, shot him in the head. Moments later, the storm hit."

"But the gunshot," said Fiddles. "We all heard it. And the door was locked from the inside."

"The door was locked," I said. "There's no evidence one way or the other if it was locked from the inside or out, except the key which was found on the floor, after Hal had been in the room and, I noticed, stumbled as he left. He planted the key then. As for the gunshot, I suspect that was an improvisation on Rosalind's part. She couldn't have known that it would rain nor that there'd be a fire in the fireplace when she returned, but it was a welcome eventuality. While drying herself before the fire she simply dropped a rifle shell into the flames. Some random period of time later, while we were all gathered in the drawing-room, it exploded in the heat."

"It was an illusion," said Ivor. "The major had been dead for hours."

"Just so," I said. "And the only one who could have killed the major was the only one not on the premises when it occurred — Rosalind."

"He didn't kill himself," said Laetitia. "I knew he couldn't."

"Of course not, Mrs Canterfell," I said. "He had too much to live for."

A dark shadow passed over Laetitia's face, which she then turned on her son.

"Hal," she said, as though from across an open grave. "How could you?"

"No, Mother," said Hal. "It's all wrong. It's just Fairfax and his friends picking on me, like they've always done."

"We'll soon get to the bottom of this," said Ivor. "Where is Miss Pierpoint now?"

"Gone," I said. "Probably halfway to London by now."

"What?" said Ivor. "You let her go?"

"I did," I said. "Please allow me to explain why."

"I wish you would."

"I let her go, Inspector, because of you."

"Me."

"You," I said. "You were determined to hang Fiddles. We were at Eton together, Fiddles and I. We were at Oxford together. We rowed together. We were fined five pounds each for misuse of a barge in a built-up area together. Any one of those material points, on its own, makes it incumbent upon me to not only identify the real killer, but to provide you with the proof you need for a conviction as, by all indications, you would otherwise pursue an unjust case against a talented coxswain."

"How does allowing a suspect get away accomplish that?"

"Confession, Inspector," I explained. "I allowed Miss Pierpoint to leave on the condition that she admit to everything, which she did."

"That only makes it worse," said Ivor. "You let a confessed killer escape."

"Lesser of two evils, Inspector," I said. "She explained everything. This was all Hal's plan from the outset. He assured her that the hoverflies were a harmless prank, and then when they resulted in the death of Sebastian Canterfell, he had her trapped. Either she go along with the rest of his plan or, he assured her, she'd hang for murder."

"That's a diabolical lie," blurted Hal. "She's a professional. A hired killer. She's a trained bounty hunter and marksman from Arizona. The hoverflies were my idea, that bit's true, but I didn't even want to kill the major, that was all her. I wanted to wait, and make sure that Fiddles had taken his seat in the Lords, but she wanted her money now, just like an American, and insisted that we kill the major and collect on the will."

The effect was marked. This stark admission was followed by a stunned silence so deep you'd think time had stopped.

"As I was saying, Inspector," I said. "Confession. Hug, you will find Miss Pierpoint in her room, awaiting a taxi to take her to the train station."

Hal shot me a look that was sharp at both ends. "She's still here? She hasn't confessed?"

"Not yet," I said, "but I expect after she's heard how you did, in front of a roomful of witnesses, she'll realise that she has little choice. For the moment, though, she has no idea that she's been found out. I saw her earlier as she was preparing to leave, and agreed with her that she should. I told her I had figured out her game — she was a con artist, posing as a distant relative so that she might save on hotel bills while visiting England. I said that I couldn't stand by while she trifled with the affections of a friend, and so I offered to call her a taxi, which I appear to have neglected to do."

CHAPTER TWENTY

The Tantalising Twist in the Case of the Canterfell Codicil

There was something somehow inversely reminiscent of the festive yesteryears at Canterfell Hall as those of us who hadn't murdered anyone in the previous two days gathered in the foyer to see off those who had.

Fiddles, looking like a Basset Hound that had just received disturbing news from abroad, handed the keys of the Morris to Hug, whose plan was to take the prisoners to the station, there to await more official transportation to London.

"Rosalind," said Fiddles. "Only tell me to wait for you and I will."

Rosalind fixed Fiddles with a bemused expression, then said to Hug, "You'll let a sap like this run the country? God help England."

Hug moved his prisoner along and I sidled up to Fiddles.

"Probably best to not get too attached at this point, old bean," I said.

"I daresay you're right, Anty," said Fiddles. His Basset Hound droop stiffened into a resigned bearing, now more like a Beagle tied to a lamp post outside a tobacconist's, as he watched Rosalind climb into the back of the car.

"I hope you understand, Mother, I did it for us," said Hal over his shoulder as Ivor led him down the steps.

"Oh, Hal," said Laetitia, leaning on the arm of the honourable member. She took a long draw from her whisky and soda and added, "Do shut up."

Ivor accompanied Hal to the Morris and left him in the passenger seat, stood briefly with his hands on his hips, then turned to face us.

"No hard feelings I hope, Mister Canterfell."

Fiddles didn't actually say "Ha!" nor even come close to saying "Ha!", but I knew from close association as the stroke of his stern pair that "Ha!" was very much what my former coxswain had a mind to say.

"Of course not, Inspector," he said instead. "Whyever should there be?"

"You were unjustly accused and, technically, arrested for a crime you didn't commit," explained Ivor. "Oftentimes people regard that as grounds for complaint."

"I beg your pardon?" said Fiddles, scandalised.

"I say, steady on, Inspector," I said. "We're all gentlemen here. I hardly think Fiddles is going to go crying to the housemaster over a trifling thing like single-minded persecution on a capital charge."

"I should say not," confirmed Fiddles with dignity.

"Sort of thing Hal might do," I said.

"Beneath even him, I would have thought," countered Fiddles.

"I am curious by your choice of words, though, Inspector,"

I said. "If it's so that oftentimes people regard false arrest as grounds for complaint, if it's not overstepping my place, you might consider cutting back on the practice."

"Stands to reason it would reduce the number of complaints," added Fiddles.

"Just where I was going with it, yes," I said.

"Yes, fair point, well made," said Ivor. Then he said, "Gentlemen... ladies," with a curt bow, turned on his heel, and climbed into the Morris.

We watched the car crunch away down the drive and I asked, "Are you getting that back, Fiddles? I was hoping to cheat the field between here and the train station."

"Are you leaving us already, Anty?"

"Must needs, old man," I said. "I have many pressing matters in the metropolis. Not the least of which is rebuilding my flat from the inside out and sourcing a valet who won't reduce it all once again to ash. How about you? You're free to do as you please, now, up to and including painting London a vibrant hue of red."

"There are affairs need addressing here, first," said Fiddles, as one engaging a swing-voter in a doorstep interview. "I'll have to settle Grandpapa's estate, obviously, prior to assuming the earldom, at which point my first duty will be to Fray."

"I expected as much," I said. "May I offer a suggestion, then, as regards said duties?"

"Of course."

I outlined my propositions in broad strokes and Fiddles adopted them wholesale, beginning with Miss Lively, whom we called over.

"Miss Lively," said Fiddles. "You're sacked. I shall be pleased to offer you a generous settlement, but you are dismissed with immediate effect."

"But, what will I do?" mourned the former poisoner, deprived of the tools of her trade. "I know no other work."

"Arguably, Miss Lively," I said, "you didn't know this work, either. But you're not being dismissed, you're being liberated. Porter? Could you step over here a moment?"

Porter joined us and I laid out my plan before his eager ears.

"For a very brief window you have the opportunity to acquire one of the most experienced hospitality engineers in the village. Miss Lively is currently considering offers, and I have it on good authority that the integrity of Fray Wood will be maintained, so you're going to be needing all the help you can get."

"You wouldn't object to working in a tavern, Miss Lively?" asked Porter.

"Call me Dottie," said Miss Lively, smiling warmly on her new employer. "I believe I could find some satisfaction in it."

Porter and Miss Lively began their new arrangement immediately and tarried to open the Hare's Foot Tavern and Inn.

"Luna, Lydde, could you step this way, please," said Fiddles. "Luna, I hope to induce you to accept a new position at Canterfell Hall."

Luna smiled broadly at the ground. "It would be my honour to do my modest best in your kitchen, sir."

"Not merely as cook, Luna," said Fiddles. "I'm asking you to become head of staff."

"Oh, yes?" said Lydde. "And what would that make me then?"

"Subordinate," said Fiddles. "Take it or leave it."

"I'll be leaving it right where it belongs then," said Lydde. "And so will Luna."

To that Luna raised her head and drew herself to her full height, which turned out to be two or three inches more than anticipated.

"Mister Lydde," she said with a tone of authority and a soupçon of menace. "Please see to it that tea is cleared from the conservatory, and then see me in the kitchen with regards tonight's menu. I may be requiring you to visit the butcher in the village."

Lydde shot me a reproachful glance and then, in an instant, appeared to reflect on this turn of events.

"Yes, Miss," he said, and was gone.

"He just wants taking in hand," said Luna, and she, too, skipped off to the kitchen.

"I think I might stay on for a bit, Fairfax. See if I can be of any use," said Halliwell, with Laetitia at his side.

"Of course, Father," said Fiddles. "Aunt Lettie, I wonder if you would consider taking over the day-to-day management of the castle. Sort of what Uncle Sebastian was doing, except the precise opposite."

"Thank you, Fairfax. It would be my pleasure," said Laetitia, and she and the honourable member returned to the house.

"Do I understand that you're leaving us, Mister Boisjoly?" said Vickers. "Shall I prepare your bags?"

"Please do," said Fiddles. "And then, Vickers, you'll want to prepare your own. I'm very grateful for your service, but the fact is yours is a role for a younger man."

"Of course, sir," said Vickers, as though Fiddles had just asked him to serve cocktails on the terrace.

"I'm sorry to see you go, of course," continued Fiddles, "but my dear friend Anty Boisjoly has need of a top-flight valet, and in light of everything he's done for me it wouldn't quite be playing the game to deny him, you understand."

Vickers held my eye with watery recognition in his own. "Your valet, sir?"

"If it wouldn't be an imposition," I said.

"I shall pack immediately, Mister Boisjoly," he said, and turned on his heel with the energetic spring of a man half his age, whatever that might be.

A summer sun was setting over Sussex and glowing at the window of our compartment. The countryside passed us in the rich, green blur of a rural evening seen from a train, and it swirled around us in a miasma of perfumes once bucolic, then agrarian, then again the scents of groves and blossoms. It was a journey of the senses through humbling nature, and it served to remind me how much I was looking forward to returning to civilisation.

"We'll have to improvise for a few weeks, Vickers," I said. He sat across from me in the direction of travel and looked as though he was about to nod off. "I thought we might reopen the house in Kensington while I monitor repairs of the flat in Mayfair."

"Very good, sir," said Vickers. "It will be a pleasure to return to familiar quarters."

"I daresay it will," I agreed. "Helps to know where everything is."

"Manifestly so," said Vickers. "My memory isn't what it once was."

"That won't present a problem. I'm not a man of routine."

"This was also so of your father."

"I know, but that's mostly because he was rarely sober after eleven o'clock in the morning."

"I couldn't say, sir," said Vickers discreetly, "but my chief concern is my memory for faces. I confess I was relieved when you announced that Miss Pierpoint was not the young lady's real name."

"Vickers, are you familiar with the rules of Quite Right, Milord? Because if we're not playing a round right now I'm not sure that I follow your line of thinking."

"I merely mean to say that when I knew her in Kensington, it was as a Miss Penelope Shearer," said Vickers. "I feared that I was misremembering, but when it was revealed that Rosalind Pierpoint wasn't her real name, I knew that they were one and the same woman."

"Are you telling me that Miss Pierpoint knew my parents?"

"Yes, sir," said Vickers. "Your mother engaged her as a secretary to the late Mister Boisjoly. In fact, if memory serves, your father had an appointment with her at Wormwood Scrubs the day of his unfortunate accident."

Small world, I thought, and then realised that it wasn't. I recalled only then a seeming non-sequitur that Hal had uttered when I saw him that first evening. "How's your mother," he'd asked. He didn't express condolences about my own father, he'd asked after my mother, a woman of the world with friends all over it. Hal wouldn't have had the first idea how to find and negotiate terms of work with a professional assassin, but my mother probably counts dozens of them among her dearest intimates. Of course she could source an American photographer who was in reality a deadly sniper or, who knows, a valet who starts kitchen fires.

Anty Boisjoly Mysteries

This has been the first Anty Boisjoly mystery. The second is The Case of the Christmas Ghost, in which Anty Boisjoly must defend his Aunty Boisjoly against a charge of murder when she claims to have seen the cadavre on Christmas morning, hours before the victim stood his old friends a round of farewell drinks.

You can sign up for this and other fascinating bits of Boisjoly trivia here...
https://indefensiblepublishing.com/books/pj-fitzsimmons/
...and you can find The Case of the Christmas Ghost at your local Amazon dealership....
https://www.amazon.com/gp/product/B08YWS4R4P

I hope that you enjoyed reading this at least half as much as I enjoyed writing it. If you did, please don't hesitate to tell everyone you know, without spoiling how it was done, of course. If you didn't like it, then, by all means, blab it all over town.

Printed in Great Britain
by Amazon